WHOSE BED HAVE YOUR CLAWS BEEN UNDER

MONSTERVILLE, USA, BOOK 5

AVA ROSS

WHOSE BED HAVE YOUR CLAWS BEEN UNDER

Monsterville, USA, 5

Copyright © 2023 Ava Ross

All rights reserved.

No part of this book may be reproduced in any form or by any electronic or mechanical means, including information storage and retrieval systems, without written permission from the author, except for the use of brief quotations with prior approval. Names, characters, events, and incidents are a product of the author's imagination. Any resemblance to an actual person, living or dead is entirely coincidental.

Cover art by Wolfraven Studio

Editing/Proofreading by Owl Eyes Proofs & Edits

SERIES BY AVA

Mail-Order Brides of Crakair

Brides of Driegon

Fated Mates of the Ferlaern Warriors

Fated Mates of the Xilan Warriors

Holiday with a Cu'zod Warrior

Galaxy Games

Alien Warrior Abandoned

Beastly Alien Boss

Bride of the Fae

A Sci-fi Holiday Tail

Monsterville, USA

Monster on Board
(Co-written with Alana Khan)

A Monster Worth Fighting For
(Monster Between the Sheets)

Love at First Orc

Third Galaxy on the Left

You can find my books on Amazon.

WHOSE BED HAVE YOUR CLAWS BEEN UNDER?

My ex-boyfriend was transformed into a medusa, and he's set his eyes on me.

Ten years ago, I was convinced I'd one day marry my high school boyfriend, Darrow. But when a mad scientist experimented on him and others in Petrified Woods, they were changed into monsters. My parents dragged me from town before I could make sure Darrow was okay. Not long after that, they told me he was dead.

Now I'm back in Petrified Woods to be the maid of honor at a friend's wedding. And guess who's the best man?

Darrow.

He's not dead.

He's mad at me for leaving him.

And his steely gaze could turn me to stone with a single glance.

Whose Bed Have Your Claws Been Under? is a part of the Monsterville, USA Series. Each book is a standalone but best if read in order. Expect romantic hijinks with monsters, heat, and a happily ever after.

Check out the entire Monsterville world!
Candy for my Orc Boss
Orc Me Baby One More Time
Gargoyles Just Want to Have Fun
Don't Go Knotting My Heart
Whose Bed Have Your Claws Been Under?
Uptown Ogre
Oops, I Elf'd it Again
My Orc-y Breaky Heart
Hold Me Closer, Fiery Phoenix
Who Let the Demon Out?

CHAPTER 1
PAIGE

"Aw, you look gorgeous," I told my friend Monica. She stood in front of a long mirror in one of the twenty-five bedrooms in the castle venue, her slim body encased in a white wedding gown fit for a princess.

Poppy, her orc-green face tight with excitement and tension, fluffed Monica's dress and made a few last-minute alterations, though really, the dress was perfect already.

"You think so?" Monica said, her teary gaze traveling from mine to Poppy's in the mirror. "I keep seeing pictures of my mom wearing this dress when she married my dad, and now I'll wear it when I walk down the aisle and into Trevor's arms. Thank you so much for helping with the alterations, Poppy." She hugged our friend, and Poppy beamed, her cheeks darkening. "If only Mom could be here to help me get ready. If only Dad was here to walk me down the aisle, though I'm honored Gunner agreed to do so."

Gunner was Poppy's older brother and a good friend of the groom.

With Monica's mom dead, she only had me, her best friend from high school and Poppy to be with her during this wonderful moment in her life.

I carefully blotted away her tears. "None of that, now. I know crying's a common thing at weddings, but don't ruin your make-up until after you've joined Trevor at the altar."

Nodding, she bit down on her trembling lower lip and smoothed the front of her gown. It had been made of the finest silk and tulle and had intricate beading and lace along the bodice. The skirt flowed out behind her, and Poppy had promised to hold it up so it wouldn't drag on the way to the chapel.

I stepped back. "You look wonderful. Trevor's going to be the one crying when he sees you walking down the aisle."

Elisa, Monica's wedding planner, murmured an agreement from where she stood nearby.

"Thank you so much for being here with me, Paige," Monica said. "I know we only reconnected six months ago, but it means everything to me."

"There's no place I'd rather be. Now let's get to that church so you can get married," I said with a big smile.

The door opened behind us and the owner of the castle venue, Bart, a minotaur, poked his head in. "It's time." His gaze swept across us and remained on Poppy. Color climbed into his fuzzy cheeks, and his hooves drummed on the floor.

Poppy hid her grin. Those two. I shook my head. They'd been making eyes at each other since we arrived this morning. Romance appeared to be in the air for more than one couple.

Not for me. I'd had my chance ten years ago when I was sixteen but he died.

Monica latched onto my arms and hopped in place. "I'm about to become Trevor's bride!"

I was surprised when she asked me to be her maid of honor, though touched. When my family fled Petrified Woods, I never looked back. The memory of that time still haunted me.

A mad scientist kidnapping Darrow and other townspeople to experiment on them. They escaped, but they were never the same again . . .

Darrow texted me after he escaped, telling me he didn't feel right. Something was terribly wrong. He was scared.

My parents wouldn't let me go see him, stating I had to let the medical people deal with it.

It wasn't long after that we heard screams echoing through our small town and whispers of *monsters*.

My terrified parents packed up all our possessions and fled the next night. This was the first time I'd returned to Petrified Woods.

"You're gorgeous, sweetheart." Poppy fluffed Monica's veil. At her nod, Monica smiled and started toward the door.

"I'm so glad I found you on Facebook," Monica said.

As Bart opened the door all the way, I handed Monica her glorious bouquet.

"If you hadn't found me, I never would've returned to town." How could I when Darrow died? When my parents told me, I collapsed. We'd been best friends since we were little. We'd even teased each other about getting married one day. We'd only kissed, but I knew who I wanted to be with for my first time.

My dreams died along with him.

We left the room and followed Elisa down the grand staircase. Bart waited at the bottom, red capes hanging over his arm.

When we reached him, he draped one around each of our shoulders. With Poppy, he paused and loosely tied a white bow beneath her chin. He stood there, staring at her while she did the same, and I began to think we'd be gray before we arrived at the church.

"Guys," Monica said with a laugh. "Later, okay?"

Poppy blushed. Bart stumbled backward, nearly tripping when one of his hooves caught on the rug.

"I apologize," he said, giving us a bow. His hand swept out. "Please."

The chapel was located behind the castle, though the reception would be held in the grand ballroom spanning half the second floor. We crossed the foyer, continued down a hall, and paused at the rear entrance door.

Bart clomped around us and opened it.

Stepping outside, I paused on the big stone deck to suck in a breath of crisp, wintery air. Poppy juggled Monica's train, making sure it didn't fall in the snow.

Monica grinned my way, her tears gone. "I can't wait to marry Trevor."

And from what I'd seen last night at the rehearsal dinner, he felt the same.

The only person missing from the dinner had been the best man. I wouldn't meet him until the wedding, though it didn't matter. Once the wedding weekend was over and Monica and Trevor left for their honeymoon in two days, I'd drive away from Petrified Woods and never return.

"He's a medusa," Monica had whispered, though not in shock. After all, she was marrying an ogre. "He has snake-like hair that has a life of its own, though it's kind of sexy. It's silver," she'd said. "As is his skin, though that's a lighter color. He's kind of cute if sad." She'd frowned. "I think something horrible happened after he was changed, but no one's said a word about it to me. He's a sculptor and, rather ironically, he runs a statuary." She'd released a high-pitch giggle. "Get it? Gorgon. Statuary? I asked Trevor once if he poured his statues or . . . created them."

"Created them?" I'd asked.

"You know," she'd said in a hushed voice, "used his laser eyes to turn them to stone."

I wasn't sure what to believe, but I'd meet him soon. I didn't know any sculptors, let alone guys who could solidify others with a glance from their eyes.

Leaving the deck, we walked along a garden path with Bart leading.

"Everything's so beautiful," Monica exclaimed,

stroking the red bows decorating an evergreen tree. The place looked like a holiday wonderland, and I was happy for my friend. I couldn't imagine a prettier place to get married.

Sunlight filtered through the tall, spiky trees, making the light dusting of snow we'd gotten last night sparkle. The sweet essence of pine mixed with the scent of cinnamon and cloves. Birds chirped as we passed, and I expected one to swoop down and land on Monica's finger, completing the forest princess image she projected.

We walked across a small stone bridge spanning a babbling brook, pausing to watch the water trickle over rocks and gurgle where ice was starting to form.

"It's lovely here," I said.

"Thank you," Bart said, clop-clop-clopping beside me on the path. "I inherited the estate from family and decided it was the perfect place for a wedding venue." His gaze slid to Poppy, and she sidled closer to him.

"When Trevor asked me to marry him," Monica said, "I knew we had to get married here. I've ridden my bike past this place for years, dreaming of walking through the grounds and sleeping in one of the beds."

Bart gave her another bow. "We're delighted to help make your day special."

I couldn't imagine what it cost, but Trevor's family owned the country club, and Monica was a graphic designer in high demand. They could probably afford it.

Not me, but I didn't plan to get married. My heart was ripped from my chest ten years ago, and I hadn't found anyone who could step into the gap left by Darrow's death. It might be silly to mourn someone I hadn't seen for so long, but that was me, steadfast and loyal, as my mom always said. It made me a great lawyer.

We approached the big stone church, and I marveled at the stained-glass windows on either side of the two-story doors. Organ music drifted through the air. Monica wanted a traditional wedding, and the formal march would soon herald her arrival.

"Oh," Monica called out, her eyes sparkling with tears again. "It's almost time." She smiled and hugged me, then Poppy, who still juggled Monica's train.

Two staff members dressed in black suits bowed to Monica, then swept open the double doors for her to enter.

She strode inside, her head held high, and her spine stiff with pride while I scooted behind her, trying to look dignified while holding a basket full of rose petals. Without a flower girl, the job of sprinkling them on the aisle had fallen on me.

Inside the foyer, Elisa took our capes and fluffed our dresses.

We waited while the ushers approached the interior door.

Bart plodded to the right and opened a small panel, giving the signal that the bride had arrived, and the wedding could begin.

Organ music grew louder, the melody a joyous fanfare that made my heart soar along with it. Long ago, I'd planned to walk down the aisle like Monica, only

Darrow would be waiting at the altar with a big grin on his handsome face.

Bart turned to Monica. "Ready?"

She nodded solemnly. "I am."

Poppy ensured her train was perfectly smooth, then stepped around her to enter through a side door with Bart and Elisa following.

The ushers opened the door to the chapel. The music rose, almost too loud.

Easing around Monica, I stepped onto the red-carpet runner stretching between the pews, and started tossing petals, taking care not to throw too many. The basket was small, and I was supposed to hold back enough to throw onto the altar where Monica would stand with Trevor.

Peeking up, I took in Trevor gazing at Monica with complete adoration. Tears glistened in his eyes, and my heart squished for my friend. They'd be so happy together.

His best man stood to his right, though he hadn't turned to look. The silver, snake-like hair Monica had described was pulled back in a thick bunch at his nape, the long strands dangling past his shoulders. Did a person cut living hair or let it grow as long as it liked? Tall, he towered over Trevor, who was six-three. His shoulders were equally broad, tapering to a narrow waist. He had a nice butt, something I shouldn't be noticing.

Monica sniffed.

I paid attention to where I threw the rose petals.

When I reached the altar, I stepped to the side and tossed petals on the smooth surface. I waited for Monica to join Trevor in front of the reverend, then fluffed her train and made sure her gown lay smoothly. Taking her flowers, I stepped up beside her.

I glanced toward the best man, wondering what he looked like from the front. Was he as gorgeous face-to-face as he was from behind?

Shock poured through me, and I released a guttural groan.

Monica glanced my way, but I couldn't drag my eyes away from him.

Darrow.

CHAPTER 2

DARROW

Paige was back in Petrified Woods, was she? If I wasn't standing beside my best friend who was about to marry the woman he loved, I would pivot on my heel and stalk from the church.

Or stomp over to her and confront her.

Leave it to my old girlfriend—who abandoned me when I needed her most—to show her face in town once more.

I fumed, barely hearing the reverend going through the traditional vows, marrying my ogre friend to Monica. She sniffed and tears trickled down her cheeks, and it was so sweet, even I almost got caught up in the wonder.

If I believed in love, I might've, but the feeling had been stomped beneath Paige's shoe when she raced from town, fleeing in the night without saying goodbye. I waited every day at the mailbox for over a month, hoping she'd send a letter. Explain. All I got from the experience was a solid lump in my gut and a wall of hurt around my heart.

"I now pronounce you man—er, ogre, that is, I do apologize—and wife," the reverend said. "You may kiss the bride."

Trevor carefully lifted Monica's veil and cupped her cheeks. The audience sighed. Even Paige sniffed. I stood frozen beside my friend, trying not to shoot her a look that would literally turn her to stone. Could I capture the expression of shock she'd feel as her body solidified?

I should be over her by now. Nothing should hurt this much.

Yet my heart was cracking. I couldn't seem to stop it from happening.

The music started again, and Monica and Trevor rushed down the aisle, their faces wreathed with smiles. The audience cheered.

Paige remained in place, staring forward as if I truly had turned her to stone. Only her hands trembled.

The basket of rose petals she held dropped from her hands, clattering on the altar.

If I was as hardened inside as I'd hoped, I'd turn and follow my friend, leave Paige standing alone like she'd left me ten years ago. But I guess I still had a tiny bit of squishiness left inside. I stepped over to her, picked up the basket, and held it out to her.

"This is yours," I said.

"Darrow," she cried.

I didn't hear the pain in her voice. I didn't see the

shock on her face. And I didn't feel the crusty walls of my heart still cracking.

"Damn you, Paige," I hissed. "Why did you come here?"

"You're supposed to be dead!"

Of all the things I thought she might say to me, that was the last. "What the hell are you talking about?"

The reverend cleared his throat at my slur. After shaking his finger at me, he puttered about at the altar.

I glared at Paige. "Is that the best you've got?"

"You don't believe me?" she sounded horrified. Damn, but lies came easy to her. I was seeing someone I never had all those years we'd grown up together.

The rubber tip of a walking cane poked between us.

"Skedaddle, you two," Grannie Vi said. "Everyone's waiting to leave the church, and you two were supposed to follow the bride and groom. Get your rears in gear."

She wasn't my true grandmother; everyone just called her that. While she was Rylee, Gunner's wife's grannie and Trevor's great-aunt, everyone in Petrified Woods had adopted her as their own. She loved all of us equally, something almost magical to those who felt they should be scorned.

Like me.

"If we don't leave, we'll miss out on the cake," Uncle Bub said from beside her, lifting his cane to tap my spine. "That's the whole point of a wedding, isn't it?"

And he wasn't my uncle. He'd come to town for the wedding, arriving a few days ago. He and Grannie Vi were dating, though there had to be a ten year age difference between them. Not that I cared about anything like that.

"He keeps me young," Grannie confided in a too-loud whisper when she introduced us the other day.

Color had risen in his face, but he'd beamed and put his arm around her waist. Many of us could aspire to affection like that.

"Weddings are about more than cake, Bub," Grannie Vi said, shooting him a grin. "I think you know that."

I noted the new ring glistening on her left hand. Were they engaged?

"Go!" Grannie Vi herded us down the aisle with her cane, Uncle Bub hobbling along beside her.

Everyone else filed out of their pews, mingling behind us.

Outside, we paused on the front step. The sun poured down, making me sweat already. No, that was a result of seeing Paige.

Could I avoid her for the rest of the wedding weekend?

I'd asked Trevor why they weren't leaving on their honeymoon right away, and he said something about wanting to visit with us. Once they left on Monday, I would too.

"Don't hang out here," Grannie Vi said, prodding us down the steps and out onto the walkway. "Keep going, you two."

She kept at us on the path leading to the back of the castle, up the back stairs and inside, and down the hall to the foyer. There, she waved her cane to where Trevor and

Monica stood in the front parlor getting their photos taken by the fireplace. "Don't you need to get your pictures taken too?"

Probably.

Paige stoically didn't look my way. She walked across the carpet with spine-tight dignity.

"Come on, Bub," Grannie said, urging me to follow Paige. "There are party favors on the tables in the reception hall, and we need to find our seat assignment and grab what's ours before someone else steals it."

Grunting, he moved quickly behind her, aiming for the elevator that would take them to the second-floor ballroom where the reception was being held.

Inside the parlor, Gunner and Rylee stood near the windows, grinning at the wedding couple. They held hands, something I saw them doing all the time. They'd been married a few years and had a toddler son, Josh, though they'd left him with her mom. Gunner grew up in a nearby town and was a created monster like me, though he'd drank a strange brew versus the horror that had been visited upon me. Raze, Trevor's ogre wedding planner, lived in Monsterville.

Raze stood to the side, watching benignly as Monica and Trevor posed. He nudged the bridge of his glasses higher on his nose, hiding his eyes.

Elisa, one of Monica's friends, and the second wedding planner from Monsterville—I had no idea why they needed two—stood beside Raze, scowling at him rather than watching everyone else. She was human, however, not a monster.

We posed with and without the bride and groom, and my face ached from forcing a smile. Paige continued to ignore me, even when the photographer made us face each other and hold hands.

Finally, this wretched part of the day was over. Elisa steered us to the elevator and into the second-floor ballroom where everyone else sat at tables munching on appetizers.

"Head table, you four," she said with a big smile. "Bride and groom in the middle, of course, but you two will sit together on their left side."

I'd hoped we'd be separated by the happy couple.

"Right side," Raze said. He'd followed us, scowling at Elisa while the elevator lifted us to the second floor.

"Left," Elisa insisted, tension making her voice creak.

Monica and Trevor took their places.

"Right." Raze urged us closer to the table while Elisa followed, grumbling.

We ended up to the left of the happy couple, and I was grateful Elisa and Raze hadn't decided to duel it out before we took our seats.

I held out Paige's chair for her to sit. I might be a gorgon now, but I did still remember the civil graces.

She thanked me politely, and as I settled on her right, she turned to chat with Monica.

I was miffed, though I wasn't sure why. I didn't want Paige to talk to me, did I? Listening to her insist she'd thought I was dead (really?) didn't sound like my idea of a fun time.

Information like this could be looked up online. I

graduated high school, started a business, and some of my stone artwork had been featured in the Petrified Woods Gazette. If she'd Googled my name, she would've seen that I was very much alive.

I'd missed her. The scientist changed me and not in a way I could welcome. I'd needed her strength and her reassurance that everything would be okay. My mom shunned me, moving out of town, and she'd done the same. Only Dad remained by my side.

Dinner was served, and we ate. Then the band started playing, and Monica and Trevor got up to slow dance. He kissed her to the cheers of the crowd, and then Monica waved our way.

Paige and I remained in our chairs.

Monica curled her fingers our way again, her eyebrows lifting.

"I think she wants us to dance," Paige said, her voice harder than stone. If anyone knew what stone was, it was a gorgon. I could change anyone or anything into granite with one glance, though I'd finally learned to control it.

When I sighed, Paige winced. For a moment, I felt bad. I was being an asshole.

But then I remembered she'd left me when I needed her most.

CHAPTER 3
PAIGE

Why did Darrow have to be such a sexy asshole? I should be glaring at him now, not drooling about him whenever he wasn't looking my way.

He'd grown both upward and outward, though there didn't appear to be a scrap of fat on him. Nope, he could compete with a wall of muscles.

His snake-like hair only added to his appeal. His skin had taken on a silver cast when he was changed, the color of his hair was only slightly darker. His teal eyes that were the original Darrow had a gleam behind them that wasn't there before, making him even more appealing than he'd been back when we were sixteen. He was a force to be reckoned with, a guy to long for the rest of my days.

And he hated me.

I wasn't sure what to think about that. When my parents told me he died, I'd curled in a ball on my bed and sobbed for weeks. I'd only come out of my room when Mom and Dad threatened me with force-feedings.

I'd spent years mourning his loss, as if a part of me had been ripped away and buried along with him. Some say first love is the strongest, and they had to be right. Look at me, my heart squeezing tight because he'd tossed a look of anger my way.

I wanted to curl up on a bed and cry because I'd lost him all over again.

We stepped onto the dance floor, and for a second, he stared at me like he was going to reject me in front of everyone. Then he took my hand and tugged me close. We swayed together to the slow tune, and while I might be cursed for doing it, I laid my head on his chest. His heart drummed faster than it should.

If I was a girl who believed in second chances, I'd think his heart was responding to my presence. Nope. He was probably wishing he could run away and never see me again.

I wasn't going to keep pleading my case. If he didn't believe me, there wasn't anything I could do but let it go.

It hurt, and it wasn't going to get any better, but slinking away sure beat letting him reject me over and over.

I closed my eyes, swaying in tune with his body. When we were sixteen, we'd almost gone all the way. I wasn't sure why we'd stopped, and after he "died," I'd mourned that I didn't have that memory to cling to.

"Don't get into this too much," he said in a gravelly voice.

"I'm enjoying the music." My eyes stung, and I hoped I didn't cry.

To him, I epitomized betrayal. To me, he was a dream that was wrenched from my arms. It wasn't fair of fate to thrust him back into my life but still deny me the chance to be with him.

"As soon as we can do this politely, I'll go to my room," he said.

Each of us had our own room in the castle.

"You can enjoy the rest of the evening," he added. "And I'll avoid you throughout the weekend."

"That would probably be best."

Monica and Trevor had planned various activities for us. Darrow and I could get caught up in everything and find a way to avoid each other.

Or I could remain in my room, crying.

Except . . . I hadn't done anything wrong. I'd come to Petrified Woods to enjoy Monica and Trevor's wedding, and that was what I was going to do, dammit. Darrow could hide away if he wanted to avoid close contact with me.

I'd smile and . . . flirt. Yes! I'd find someone to flirt with ASAP and show Darrow I didn't need him in my life to feel complete. I'd survived his death; I could make it through his rejection.

Why did it hurt so much, then?

He gave me a curt nod, and I returned it.

The song ended, and we returned to our table. As I sat, my phone buzzed. I scrolled in to see who was calling, only to huff Darrow's way.

This should be interesting.

I answered the call. "Hi, Mom and Dad!"

CHAPTER 4
DARROW

I started to rise to leave Paige to talk with her parents without me hanging on every word, but she latched onto my wrist and held me in my chair.

She was tiny compared to me. If I wanted to leave, I'd do so, and she could just deal.

But I remained where I was.

"I told you, remember?" Paige said into the phone. "I'm at my old friend, Monica's, wedding. We reconnected on Facebook. I'm putting you on speakerphone, okay?" She switched the call, though I had no idea why. I'd liked her parents well enough, but I didn't feel the need to chat with them today.

"I don't believe you mentioned a wedding this weekend," her mom, Francine, said. Paige's dad, Franklin, murmured agreement in the background.

"Yes, Monica and Trevor, though you don't know him," Paige said. "You must remember Monica, though.

We were good friends in high school. We played on the same field hockey team."

I could almost taste Francine's shock in the air. "Monica . . . lives where?"

"Oh, she never left Petrified Woods."

"Please tell me you're not back in that wretched town," Francine shrieked so loudly, Grannie Vi turned and shook her cane our way.

"I'm in Petrified Woods, Mom," Paige said softly. "And I ran into an old friend. You might remember *him* too."

The silence through the line was only broken by what sounded like a sob.

"No. Please," Francine said in a croaky voice.

"Darrow's sitting right next to me. Funny, while he looks different from what I remember, he's anything but dead."

"I knew we should've been honest with her," Franklin grumbled. "But no, you wanted to tell her he died."

"We had no choice," Francine said.

"How could you do that to me, Mom? Dad?" Paige's stark gaze met mine. "He was my friend, and you stole him from me."

Franklin huffed. Francine started sobbing.

"Don't be too harsh with us," Franklin finally said. "We did what we thought was best."

I slumped in my chair, completely defeated. I'd clung to my anger at Paige, fortifying the wall with scorn when . . . She was telling me the truth.

"I'm going to hang up now," Paige said, tears on her cheeks. They made her beautiful green eyes glisten. Her auburn hair had been swept up and secured on the back of her head, making her neck look as lovely as a swan's. I was stunned when I saw her standing at the end of the aisle.

I was equally stunned now.

"Please don't hang up with anger," Francine said softly. "Please, Paige. We only did what we thought was right."

"You made my choice for me!" Paige gouged at her phone, missing at first, then hitting the disconnect button.

I gaped at her, seeing her for what felt like the first time. She . . . hadn't lied.

"So, do you think I set that up?" she said, rising. "Do you think I somehow got my mom to cry and state she lied about your death, that I made my dad do it as well?" Her hands flew up into the air. "Probably." She pressed her face close to mine. "Well, you can live with your anger, Darrow. I'm done with it."

She didn't wait for me to speak, though I sputtered, struggling to overcome my shock long enough to make my tongue work.

Pivoting on her heel, she fled, darting out of the ballroom.

I was a fool.

Leaping to my feet, I took off after her.

CHAPTER 5

PAIGE

I swept from the ballroom and raced down the huge front staircase, nearly breaking my leg and falling when my heel caught on the carpet. Once I reached the foyer, I fled to the back door, snatched one of the red velvet capes off a hook, and bolted outside.

"Paige, wait," Darrow cried from behind me.

I kept running. I was done. Way past done. I'd let him hear the truth, and he sat there, staring at me. He still didn't believe me. Well, who needed him? Not me. Not me!

Tears streamed down my face, making it hard to see the path. I lost track of where I was and somehow ended up behind the church. Spying a tall hedge maze ahead, I lumbered up the hill and darted through the arched opening.

Darrow's footsteps rang out behind, but he'd give up and return to the party. I could make my way to the center of the maze and hide. No one would expect me to make an appearance until morning. Monica and Trevor, so in love, would be busy together. She sure wouldn't need her maid of honor.

I took a right inside the maze and raced to the end, where I went left. Ha, this was easy. Hopefully not so easy that Darrow could follow. Partway down the next passage, I came to an intersection. Spying a dead end ahead, I turned left. I wove through the maze, turning this way and that, and even once found myself exiting the back side of the maze, though I turned around and trotted back inside again.

"Paige," Darrow called from somewhere behind me. "Where are you?"

"Not where you'll find me," I whispered, turning at each corner, snaking my way toward the center of the maze.

Crashes rang out to my right, followed by groans, but he sounded lively enough that I didn't feel the need to turn back and make sure he was alright. He'd survived his supposed death already. I doubted the maze would attack him.

Finally, the sounds behind me faded, and I emerged into the center of the maze. About twenty-by-twenty, and peppered with tall statues, they'd placed a pretty fountain in the center of the open area. Winter had been warm this year, and the water danced, sparkling in the twinkle lights they'd strung around the area. Truly, it was a gorgeous location. Too bad my mood didn't match the lovely place.

I strolled on the path edging the outer part of the

clearing, taking in the small flower beds dusted with snow. Even here, they'd kept the festive atmosphere going with holly adorned with bright red berries. Eventually, I sank onto a wooden bench, leaning back to watch the nymph fountain spray water upward from her open mouth. She held her hands up poetically, her face tilted toward the sky.

Clouds parted overhead, and moonlight shone down. The water glistened, and the trickle should be enough to soothe even the weariest bones. Instead, I churned inside.

Maybe I should've waited to hear what Darrow had to say.

No, no. I wasn't that much of a sucker.

But he was alive, something I'd prayed for since I was told he'd died.

"Paige? I know you're in here. Let me know where you are." Desperation came through in his voice. "Let me know you're safe!"

Safe from what? This wasn't a monster's hunting grounds, though monsters did live in the area. It was Petrified Woods, the infamous home of monsters *created* by a scientist more monstrous than those he experimented on. The monsters living in the rest of the world now had been born that way.

Just because I didn't want to see Darrow didn't mean I was dangling precariously off the side of the castle, ready to slip and tumble to my death.

More crashes rang out. Really, wasn't he going to give up?

I had to admire his persistence even if it irked me. It hurt that he hadn't believed me, that he'd needed my parents' convenient phone call to convince him. I thought we'd been better friends than that. While I was thrilled he was still alive, I couldn't reconcile my excitement with his disbelief.

"Paige? I'm not giving up."

My lips thin, I shook my head. He could wait until tomorrow; allow the steam still blasting from my ears to blow away. Then I might actually be willing to speak to him in a pleasant manner.

Or not.

Twigs and branches crackled as he made his way through the maze. Was he taking the paths or crashing straight through? I almost wanted to call out to him just to keep him from destroying the pretty maze.

Scraps and mangled curses rang out as I assumed leaves and stems ripped at his clothing. A tragedy right there; I imagined he'd rented the tux and would need to pay for any damage.

Birds shot up into the sky not far away, and I braced myself. If nothing else, Darrow never gave up. Back when we were younger, he'd bang his head against a wall until it fell and prod me until I joined him in whatever he wanted to do. Like jumping off the railroad tracks into the lake, something I'd been squeamish about doing. He took me tandem parasailing on that same lake, and while I'd been scared to do it at first, I was willing as long as he held my hand. Funny, but he was the one who was nervous as we soared through the sky while I pointed and exclaimed about everything we saw.

We'd shared our first kiss while floating through the sky. The memory made my chest tighten.

He'd died not long after that.

And now he was alive.

I closed my eyes, trying to shut out the tears trickling down my face. My emotions tumbled through me. Everything I'd ever wished for had come true, but instead of rejoicing in it, we'd argued.

"I'm coming, Paige," he yelled from not far away. "I'm not letting you go. Please!" He clawed his way to the top of a wall encircling the center. Spying me sitting on the bench near the fountain, he released a grim smile. "There you are." Standing, his arms spiraled to hold his balance. When his feet started to sink into the hedge, branches snapped.

He plunged forward, landing hard on his belly on the top of the hedge. His grunt rang out. Momentum kept him going, as did the hedge that gave way on my side of the wall. He fell headfirst into the center, flopping over to land with a solid thud on his back.

Only the trickling fountain echoed in the small open area.

I stood. "Darrow?"

Oh, shit. He'd died again.

I raced around the fountain and ran over to where he lay on the ground.

He wasn't moving. Had I ruined the one chance we had to start over?

When I dropped to my knees beside him, I laid my palm on his chest. Did his heart still beat? I couldn't tell. "Darrow? Please, Darrow!" I bent forward to press my ear against his chest.

He latched onto me and rolled us until I lay beneath him. Holding me tight, he braced himself up over me. "You are going to listen to me."

CHAPTER 6

DARROW

"Like you listened to me?" Paige said sharply, her breasts heaving.

I shouldn't be noticing anything like that, but jeez, she'd grown into a gorgeous woman. I might've been angry with her before, but even then, I'd noticed.

She grabbed my sleeves and yanked. "Let me up."

"I'm sorry." I sucked in a breath and pushed it out. "Stay here just a second, would ya?" If I had to pin her in place to get her to listen, it would be worth it.

Everything was at stake here. All the dreams I'd had, the ones I'd learned to stomp on until they'd sunk deep beneath the ground, were finally coming true.

She narrowed her gaze on my face. "Okay, talk. I'll listen."

"See, if I could take it back, I would. You must know what a shock it was for me to see you in the church."

"For me too. I thought you were dead, Darrow. Dead!" The emotion in her voice was real, and it stabbed through me. I thought she left me, but she'd been told I had died. How would I have handled something like that if our positions were reversed?

And I knew why they'd taken her. I'd done something horrible. Who knows what I might've . . .

Shoving aside the thought, I held eye contact with Paige. My thick bands of hair had come loose from their binding. They wove around my head, mirroring the agitation churning through me. "The moment I saw you standing at the end of the aisle, I was struck by lightning. I could barely think. Speak. Function. I couldn't believe you'd returned to Petrified Woods after running away."

"You know I didn't run." Defeat came through in her voice. Did she think I was still mad at her? I'd heard what her mom said, the inflection in her words. They'd fuckin' lied to her.

"I knee-jerk reacted because I was afraid," I said softly.

What if she wouldn't believe me? I got a taste of how she must've felt when I rejected her on the altar, and I didn't like it. She'd been quite gracious, all things considered. "I fell back on the anger that had spiked through me when you left. I thought you'd abandoned me, but now I see your parents abandoned both of us."

She slumped. "It was horrible, but I imagine you felt just as bad."

"You were alive. I had that, even if I was mad at you for leaving and never reaching out."

"It took me years to start moving forward. I kept turning, expecting to find you beside me. I'd start to tell you something or ask you to help me with my homework, but you wouldn't be there. The empty silence of the place you took at my side haunted me."

"We've both been hurt by their actions, but we were innocent." I levered myself up and off her, then reached down to help her stand. She accepted my help; I was grateful for that, but she scooted away from me. She strode around the fountain and sunk down on the bench she'd taken before.

I walked over and joined her, smoothing my hair out of my face. They had minds of their own, mostly, though they thankfully didn't voice any opinions. Nope, they just flung themselves around at the most inconvenient times, drawing attention I did my best to ignore.

"You're a gorgon," she said, studying my hair. "I've only read about medusas." When her finger got close, one of the strands looped around her finger. It stroked her fingertip, and she laughed. "It tickles."

My hair was more than happy to show feelings I didn't dare give voice to.

"I've met lots of monsters, but never a gorgon," she said.

"I don't know if gorgons exist outside of myth."

"Well, there's you. You're not a myth."

I shrugged. "I was twisted by that scientist, not born this way, as you know." I lifted my chin, daring her to reject me, this time for real. "I'm the full package." My words came out with a touch of the shock I'd felt right after I was changed. "It was horrible at first." I lifted my hand, tapping beside my left eye. "I . . ."

Do not tell her what happened.

She gazed at me with only sympathy, something no one gave me at first and with good reason.

"I eventually learned to accept this body." And to control my eyes. If I hadn't, my fellow townsfolk would've killed me, incarcerated me, or driven me from Petrified Woods.

"It must've been scary."

"I eventually figured things out." That was as close as I wanted to come to telling her about what happened back then.

Her head tilted. "What do you mean?"

"I run a statuary."

Her breath jerked inward. "That's . . ."

"Funny, right? A gorgon selling statues for people to place in their gardens. I buy wood carvings from a woman in town and turn them into stone. You'd be surprised what I can do with plastic."

"That sounds amazing."

"And I also do stone carving." I was gushing, but I didn't care. This was Paige, my best friend, sitting beside me as if she'd never left, as if we'd ended one conversation then begun another. "The stone speaks to me, telling me what it wants to be."

"What do you do with your art?"

"I sell some of it. Others I place in gardens around town. Everyone seems to enjoy them, and that makes me happy." I didn't mention that I'd made my fortune already. My statues had gained a reputation no one could match, and celebrities were willing to pay a fortune to have just the right statue carved in their honor.

"I'm glad you've taken something some would find a challenge and turned it into a thriving career."

"What about you, Paige? What have you been up to?"

"I'm a lawyer. I finished school a few years ago. I have a ton of debt, but you know how it is. Mom and Dad have helped, though I plan to take over the payments soon."

"Where do you work?"

"In Monsterville."

I'd heard of the town where many monsters had settled, including Gunner and Rylee. They'd moved from Petrified Woods months ago.

"Most of the monsters there are real," Paige said.

Even I hadn't known there truly were monsters. They'd lived a parallel life from humans, some adopting human ways, others sticking strictly to their own cultures.

When monsters crept out of the woods and from beneath the ground, humans reacted with shock and dismay, feelings I well understood since I felt them about myself for a very long time. A treaty was formed, and now they lived all over the world, though a large portion of them resided in and around Monsterville. I heard they felt welcome there. I hadn't visited the town.

"I joined a practice there," Paige said.

We watched the fountain for a long while, but the silence between us felt healing, not upsetting.

"Where do we go from here, Darrow?" she asked softly.

"Where would you like to go next, Paige?" When I was sixteen, I was in love with her. I'd grown up since then, and my goals were different. If she'd remained in town, I could easily see us still together. But now?

"I don't know." She turned to face me. "Ten years ago, I knew what I wanted."

"Me." I didn't need to ask. She'd felt the same as I had.

"Now everything's changed. I'm glad you're alive." Reaching out, she took my hand.

I wanted her back in my life for always. I'd accept friendship, but my heart . . . How could I still be half in love with this woman? It could be the dream of who she'd been back when we were young. My entire life had formed around her.

But if she felt differently than me, I'd have to let her go. Although, I was never one to give up easily.

"Tell you what," I said, my voice husky with emotion, "give me this weekend to convince you we deserve a second chance."

"At what? What do you want from me, Darrow?"

Naming it could break the tiny thread still stretching between us. I couldn't risk losing her again.

"We've changed a lot since you left town," I said. Hopefully for the better, though some might argue about that now that I was a gorgon.

"We're older. Maybe we're not who we were back then."

"We can put what happened behind us and begin anew."

"I live in Monsterville. You live here."

"It's less than an hour's drive away." Other people made long-distance relationships work.

Would I consider leaving the town I'd lived in since I was changed into this cursed gorgon form? I never thought I'd be able to leave, that no one outside of this town would accept me. But monsters were everywhere now. I could fit in almost anywhere.

"What are you asking for?" she asked, her voice shining with the hope blooming inside my heart.

"Let's get to know each other again. Maybe by Monday, we'll be able to tell if we have something worth fighting for."

Biting her lower lip, she pinched her eyes shut, though only for a moment.

When she opened them again, they glistened with tears. "Alright, Darrow. Let's see where this goes over the weekend."

CHAPTER 7

PAIGE

Letting Darrow into my world could result in a lot of hurt. He was right that we'd changed. We weren't the same people we'd been back then, and it wasn't only because he was a gorgon.

Our careers had taken us in different directions. I wasn't surprised when he mentioned working with stone. What else could a medusa do? His eyes didn't meet mine when he talked about his past, and I sensed there were secrets there he wasn't ready to share.

We all did things we regretted. We were human, and at his core, that's who Darrow still was. The guy I'd grown up with and had such an incredible crush on when we were teenagers.

I admired him greatly. He'd taken what most would consider a curse and turned it into something admirable. A job that he not only enjoyed but one that had value.

I wasn't sure how I would've responded if I'd been

kidnapped along with him and changed into something monstrous.

Gunner's sister, Poppy, seemed to love being an orc, though she came from a town where monsters were created when they drank a brew. She dressed in what I called Disney attire and flaunted her green skin and orc shape. Given a choice, I doubted she'd change back.

Darrow was still my childhood friend, and that was all that mattered. I liked how he looked now. It was hard to keep from stroking his silver face and letting his hair coil around my fingers.

As we walked through the maze holding hands, a feeling of promise bloomed inside me.

For the first time since I saw him standing at the altar, I could fully rejoice in him being alive. Life had handed me a second chance, and I was going to cling to it, milking everything I could from this weekend.

Partway down one of the paths weaving through the maze, I stopped and looked around. I was convinced the opening on the left led back to the center, though I wasn't sure.

"Didn't we already walk this way?" I asked.

He shrugged. "I have a crappy sense of direction."

"Oh, my yes, I remember when you got lost going into town to buy my fourteenth birthday gift."

He squirmed. "I didn't exactly get lost back then. I ran into a friend, and he wanted to go fishing. Next thing I knew, we were standing on the bank of the lake reeling in bass, exclaiming about how huge they were."

I scowled, placing a fist on my hips. "You told me you got lost."

"I, um, kinda did." I believed his solemn tone until I noted the sparkle in his teal eyes.

"You lied to me," I said, unable to believe it.

His arm went around my waist, and he tugged me close. I should fight this gesture sixteen-year-old Darrow had never used. It was a man thing, and man things led to . . . Well, we all knew the answer to that.

"I caught a fish, and I brought it home for your birthday, didn't I?" he said. "I even removed the scales and cleaned out the guts."

"You know I don't like fish." I scrunched my nose at him. "I can't believe you did that, and I can't believe you didn't spill the beans and tell me you messed up."

"I crushed on you awfully bad back then, Paige." Only sincerity came through in his voice. "I didn't want to disappoint you."

I wanted to ask if he'd had a crush on anyone else since, but it would be wrong of me to ask. He thought I left him, and it was only right he move on with someone new.

Oh, shit, wait.

"You're not, like, married or anything, are you?" I squirmed out of his arms and backed up until I ran into the shrub wall.

"Do you think I'd be asking for another chance if I was?" His snake hair flicked sideways, standing out straight. Huh. Did they always do that when he was agitated? I'd have to watch to see if this was an emotional tell.

"No, not really. I figured I should ask."

"I'm not married. I haven't been with anyone for a while."

Fair enough. "Me either."

"Good," he said pertly.

"Good," I echoed just as pertly.

"I think we need to take that path," I said, pointing to an intersection ahead, partway between here and the end of the aisle.

"Lead the way, my lady," he said, sweeping the tails of his black suit jacket out, giving me a deep bow.

"Follow me." I strode past him, and he scooted to keep up, trailing his fingers down my spine. I shot him a dark glance. "Touchy-feely, aren't you?"

His hands lifted as if he'd been burned. "Would you rather I didn't touch?"

I couldn't very well say no, now could I?

CHAPTER 8

DARROW

We eventually found our way out of the maze, and by the time we'd made our way back to the main path that would take us to the castle, it was not only snowing, but a chilly wind swirled the flakes around us like mini twisters.

Paige clung to her long red cape, tugging it up to her chin.

I stopped her on the path and tugged off the wool coat I wore over my suit. "Let's put this around you."

"Oh, no, then you'll be cold."

I buttoned it up and tugged up the collar. I wanted to kiss her pink nose, but I was afraid she's smack me. Maybe not smack me, but scowl. I'd already teased her with my touch enough for tonight.

Snowflakes landed on Paige's hair, glistening like diamonds in the lights. I'd never seen anyone as gorgeous as this woman, and until the day I died, I knew I never would again.

While I should try to hold myself back, incredible longing filled me. I wanted to step right back into where we'd left off when we were sixteen and contemplating going all the way.

But I also wanted to treasure this path of rediscovery I'd set foot on with the woman Paige was today.

"Thank you," she said. "I really think you should keep your coat, however."

"I'll get it back," I said breezily. Taking her hand, I urged her down the path toward the castle.

The enormous stone building glowed with yellow lights. When I first saw it this morning, I barely held in my smirk. They'd decked it with wreathes and red bows, and even a big manger scene out front. Huge pretend presents had been stacked on the decks encircling the building, and the decorated trees out front would make it fit in well at Disney.

But I'd been touched by the beauty of Trevor and Monica's ceremony. Bart, the minotaur who owned the castle, had put a lot of time into making sure it was perfect.

There was something magical about this time of year, and it was only enhanced by the wonder of the castle partly buried in snow. Although, that feeling might be boosted by seeing Paige again.

We reached the back steps and climbed them to the deck. Inside, we left her cape and my coat on pegs and took the back staircase up three floors to where the guest rooms were located.

Her steps lagged as we reached the top, and she paused on the landing to catch her breath.

"Maybe I should carry you next time," I told her.

Screwing up her face, she scowled. "Why?"

"Because you're, um," I really should stop now, though in addition to a lack of direction, I also wasn't wise, "because you're short of breath."

"I am not." She eased past me and stomped down the hall. Rooms lined both sides. Mine was on the end, but she stopped halfway down.

"You're right," I said, holding up my palms. "You're not short of breath at all."

Turning to face me, she poked my chest. "Why aren't you short of breath?"

"I lift stone for most of the day, carrying it around."

"Do you go for runs in the woods with it?"

I sensed a trick in this question. "No," I said slowly, frowning.

"Then maybe you need to work out some more."

"Why?" I asked her the same question she'd just asked me.

She unlocked her door with the ancient key she'd taken from her pretty green gown's pocket and swung the panel open. Stepping inside, she turned, bracing the palm of her hand on the doorframe. "Did you ever consider I might be short of breath because I'm with you, Darrow?" Her lips curled up in a devilish smile.

Hell, yeah, I liked that idea.

I stepped forward to show her how much, but she swung the door closed.

CHAPTER 9

PAIGE

Darrow and I were acting like we were fifteen all over again, as if we'd regressed back to the time when we both first started noticing we liked each other. Prior to that, we were best buds playing in the dirt when we were little, riding bikes all over town as we grew older, then going swimming or just hanging out when we became teenagers.

Awareness spiked through my fifteen-year-old body, and it was heightened whenever I was around my friend. At first, I didn't know what it meant.

When I figured it out, I worried my crush on him would drive a wedge between us.

I'd spent most of my time snarling, which he had no clue meant I liked him, and he'd spent his time dropping one tease after another.

Here we were again, me snarling, him teasing. Would we advance to the time when we were sixteen and accepted that we liked each other?

Perhaps we'd know by the end of the weekend.

Because I wanted to know what he was doing in the hall, I peered through the peephole in the door. He wasn't standing outside, so I creaked open the panel an inch, poking my nose out.

He strolled down the hall and stopped at a door on the end. After unlocking it, he entered, shutting it behind him.

No glance my way.

I wasn't sure why that made me feel miffed. Unless I was still locked at age fifteen.

Grumbling, I shut the door. I crossed the room fit for a princess and entered the private bathroom, taking in my equally princess-like appearance in the mirror. Half of my hair arrangement had slipped out of the thousands of bobby pins and two cans of hairspray the beautician had used this morning. My cheeks blazed bright pink, and my lips looked as rosy as if they'd been kissed.

No such luck.

I stripped, carefully laying my gorgeous green gown on a chair in my room, tugged out the rest of the bobby pins, and stepped into the shower, savoring the hot, steamy spray on my body.

After, I dressed in PJs and climbed into bed.

Tomorrow was a big day, and I couldn't wait to get started.

I laid back and drifted to sleep, and in all honesty, I spent the night having hot dreams about what a grown-up Darrow might do with his fingers, bands of hair, and his . . .

WHEN I WALKED into the dining room the next morning, I paused in the doorway, taking in how beautiful each room in this castle was.

Lush evergreen garland with bows had been draped artfully along the top of each wall, and matching garland decorated the buffet table set up on the left side of the room.

Monica sat beside Trevor, feeding him and giggling while he kept stealing kisses. Gunner and Rylee sat nearby, doing the same.

And Raze, Trevor's cousin and personal wedding planner, sat on his right, staring forlornly at Elisa. He nudged his glasses higher on his nose, watching her with longing. Until yesterday, I hadn't seen an ogre dressed in a suit—or wearing glasses for that matter—but he looked great with his bronze skin and big horns jutting up and across his head.

I'd wondered how having two wedding planners would turn out. Elisa and Monica were friends, and she'd chuckled when I asked her how Trevor and Elisa were handling what some might see as competition. Monica just laughed and said they both better behave.

Elisa stared at her plate of half-eaten food, oblivious to the thoughtful glances Raze shot her way.

Despite our friends arriving before me for breakfast, there were still plenty of places at the enormous table.

Poppy waved from where she sat beside her older

brother, Gunner, rolling her eyes at his and his wife's antics.

"Waiting for me?" Darrow asked by my ear, joining me in the arched entrance of the room. His warm breath coasted across the bare skin of my neck, making me shiver in a delicious way no one else had ever done. Turning, I found him dressed in a button up flannel shirt and weathered jeans that clung to his muscular thighs.

After spending the night salivating over what it would feel like to trace my fingertips across each of his ripcord muscles, I'd decided I didn't want to act like I was fifteen any longer. Nope, it was time to speed this forward to at least eighteen and the legal age of consent.

So instead of acting irksome like last night, I gave him a sweet smile. "Actually, I *was* waiting for you."

He blinked, no doubt expecting me to respond in a way appropriate to his teasing. Maybe shoot him down or huff and stalk away.

Taking his hand, I dragged him over to the buffet.

"I'm starved. I need food," I said.

"Well, we can't have that. You need to eat up." He handed me a plate and waved for me to go ahead of him. "Today will work up your appetite."

Pausing while lifting a scoop of scrambled eggs to drop on my plate, I shot him a frown. "I assumed we'd be playing cards or sitting in the parlor doing puzzles."

"I thought you and I could build a snowman and go sledding."

Bart stood at the end of the table, his attention focused on Poppy, who was staring right back at him.

Today, she wore a dress just like one you'd see on Snow White, and she looked as pretty as a princess. Really, them hooking up would be a dream come true for her. She'd fit right in with living in a castle.

"Do you think a snowman fits with the ambiance of this place?" I asked Darrow, keeping my voice low.

He shrugged. "I like snowmen. They're like ice statues. If you're worried, we could build it behind the chapel."

"Alright," I said. "I'm up for making a snowman. I'm not sure about sledding. I didn't bring a lot of warm clothing with me."

"I'll keep you warm."

I rolled my eyes and continued through the buffet, taking bacon and a croissant. Turning, I walked to the table and placed my plate on the surface.

"Coffee or tea?" one of the servers asked, gliding in beside me holding two carafes.

"Tea, black, if you have it."

"Of course," she sniffed. "I'll bring you a selection of black teas. We only use full leaf here, and I'll be happy to help you select the variety you find most pleasing and prepare it for you." Turning, she strutted across the room.

"I'll have coffee," Darrow called out to her back, his hand lifted.

Another server rushed over, also leaden with carafes. "Cream, sir?" He poured coffee into Darrow's cup.

"Black," Darrow said.

The server dipped his head forward and backed

away, taking the carafes to Gunner and Rylee, filling their cups.

We sat, and I'd just placed my napkin on my lap and lifted my fork when the woman returned with a basket full of tea tins.

"Would you like to explore each sample?" she asked, winking at Darrow.

He kept his gaze trained on me, placing an arm on the back of my chair. "What do you think?"

I leaned close to him. "I just want black tea."

"Select one," Darrow told the woman.

"Oh, surely you'd like to smell this one." She unscrewed a lid and held it out to Darrow.

"He's drinking coffee," I said. "I'm the one who wants tea. Black tea."

"Or this one?" She covered the first and opened the second, tucking it beneath his nose. "The hints of cinnamon in this one is amazing. We have others, too, some with orange notes. We stock the best tea in the world."

"I want black tea," I said patiently.

"*Black* tea," Darrow repeated. His fingertips stroked my nape, and I lost all train of thought. "Princess?"

"Princess?" the woman asked, shooting me a look full of distain, topping it with lifted eyebrows. "I doubt she's royalty."

"You haven't heard of the Kingdom of Verilia?" Darrow said, somehow looking down his nose at her despite him sitting and her standing. "Princess Paige is heir to the throne."

The woman blinked slowly. "No, I haven't heard of Verilia." She shot a glance at Bart, who was glowering in our direction, and panic filled her eyes. "I'm sorry, Princess." She dipped forward in a bow, then followed it up with a curtsy. "Black tea, Your Highness?" Grabbing one of the tins, she lifted it. "You might enjoy this one. Can I prepare it for you, Your Royalness?" Not a hint of sarcasm came through in her voice. She truly seemed to believe I was the Princess of Verilia.

I placed my hand on Darrow's knee. "Um, Darrow—"

"That will be fine," he told the server in a snooty voice, lifting one of the tins. For whatever reason, he'd taken on a British accent, and it was all I could do not to snicker. "If you could be so kind, please prepare a pot of this variety for the princess."

"Very well, sir," the woman said, snatching up the basket. She bowed again, backing away while bent forward. Her pleading gaze fell on me. "Right away, Your Eminence."

As she fled through the door at the end of the room, Darrow grinned and waved to my plate. "So, how are those eggs?"

CHAPTER 10

DARROW

There wasn't anything I enjoyed more than having fun—except having fun with Paige. All teasing and princess jokes aside, I couldn't wait to spend every waking moment with her.

We ate, and she enjoyed her tea. The tea lady and another staffer whispered in the corner, their gazes shooting our way. I figured it wouldn't be long before my princess tease was revealed.

Grannie Vi and Uncle Bub strolled into the room, filled their plates, and sat with us, making our small party complete.

"Where's Josh this weekend?" Grannie Vi asked.

"My mom has him for the weekend," Rylee said, leaning against Gunner. "We love our son to pieces, but it's nice to be alone every now and then."

Gunner kissed her, his lips lingering on hers, and I envied my friend. He'd crushed on Rylee for months before they finally connected at Grannie Vi's eightieth birthday party. They'd married not long after that and Josh was soon on the way.

"Before you all take off," Monica said, rising, then clinking her spoon on her water glass. "We have some activities planned for the day." While excited chatter broke out in the room, she grinned, urging Bart to step forward.

"Exactly," he said, smoothing his white mane off his shoulders. Tufts of fur the exact same color stuck up from the collar of his shirt and from the ends of his sleeves.

Like Poppy, he'd embraced the new form he received after he was kidnapped along with me. He told me his hooves were much better than feet because he could trot outside without getting cold or putting on shoes. And he thought his horns were majestic.

Seeing some of my friends easily accept their monster shapes helped me feel the same about turning into a gorgon, despite my rocky start.

At least the scientist was captured, and we were freed —even if it was too late to change us back.

"First up is a snow sculpture contest out back," Bart said.

Monica clapped and jumped around. "Who's up for that?"

"It sounds fun," Paige said, her eyes gleaming. "We might have to postpone making a snowman, though, Darrow."

"Later?" I placed my hand over hers. She'd left it on my knee, and I'd been totally distracted since.

"I believe you'll have an advantage being a stone sculptor."

"You were the artsy one growing up."

"To make it a bit competitive," Trevor said, rising to stand with his new wife. He put his arm around her and kissed the top of her head. "We're dividing you into teams. There are only six of us here for the weekend festivities, but I've convinced Elisa and Raze to participate in all the activities. Elisa coordinated Monica's part of the wedding, and she's like family. I wouldn't want my cousin, Raze, to miss out."

Raze dipped his head forward, though his attention never left Elisa's face.

Elisa huffed but didn't say anything, which made Raze scowl.

"The only one without a partner is Poppy," Bart said. "So, if you don't mind, I'll join in as well to stand with her."

Poppy grinned. Monica jumped around some more, squealing.

"Five couples competing as teams," Monica said, turning to give Trevor a quick kiss. She eased back, beaming at us. "Doesn't this sound amazing?"

I grinned, liking where this was going. Paige's sunny expression told me she felt the same.

Elisa scowled at Raze and crossed her arms on her ample chest. His face flushed, and he looked down at his empty plate.

I'd sensed tension between them from the moment I

arrived. Maybe they didn't like being forced to share wedding planning duties.

"My castle staff has mounded snow behind the castle," Bart said. "Each couple will have a set of tools to work with. Please take care with them. We wouldn't want anyone to get hurt."

"And they've included liquid color to paint our creations," Monica said.

"We have a great prize for the winning team," Trevor said, wiggling his thick unibrow. Monica snickered.

Grannie Vi cackled and leaned over Paige to whisper to me. "I might've tucked a treat into the prize package when they weren't looking."

"No," Rylee groaned, covering her face.

Gunner grinned; his eyes gleaming. "We should win, don't you think, love?" he said softly to Rylee.

Grannie Vi's laugh grew louder.

"That's so sweet of you," Paige told Grannie Vi. When I snorted, she turned a frown my way, lowering her voice. "It'll be cookies or something like that, right?"

"Do you know much about Grannie Vi?" I asked, whispering by Paige's ear so the elderly lady wouldn't overhear.

Paige shook her head. "I've only chatted with her a few times in town. She's a kind old lady and everyone loves her."

That was true.

"Gunner and Rylee connected during Grannie Vi's birthday bash. She held games, and Rylee and Gunner won the big prize."

Paige smiled. "That sounds cute. I bet it was a lot of fun."

"I'm never going to ask." At her frown, I winked. "Grannie's a retired sex therapist."

Paige's jaw dropped, and her giggle burst out. "Oh, I get it." She laughed harder, tears streaming down her cheeks.

When everyone looked our way, she slapped her hand over her mouth, which did nothing to hide the twinkle in her pretty eyes.

I leaned closer to her, stroking her nape with my fingertips. "Let's just say Rylee blushed while Gunner told me the story. They took the box full of prizes to their room, and when they emerged in the morning . . ."

"Whoa," Paige said, shooting Rylee and Gunner a grin.

"Everyone finish up and get dressed in your warmest clothing," Monica said. "Meet us behind the castle. This is going to be so much fun!" Holding hands, she and Trevor left the room.

Gunner stood and when Rylee walked around the back of her chair, he swooped her up, tossed her over his shoulder while she squealed, and stomped from the room.

"They might be a bit delayed," Grannie Vi told me with a wink. "But that means you and Paige have a better chance of winning the prize." She stood and tightened her grip on her cane. "I think we should supervise from an upper level, don't you, Bub? There might be a few party favors left in the ballroom, and we can raid them. We can drag chairs over to the window and have a sit."

The older gentleman rose and grabbed his own cane, pointing it toward the open doorway. "Lead away, sweetheart. Lead away."

They hobbled from the room.

Raze looked at Elisa one more time, but she studiously stared at her plate. As if he'd come to a decision, he rose and stalked from the room. "Join me out back," he bit out in her direction as he left.

Elisa's face twisted. She got up and, with a sigh, hurried after him.

"My lady?" Bart said to Poppy. He extended his hoof to help her from her chair. Blushing, she took it, standing. "What do you think we should create from our mound of snow?" They walked together toward the open doorway.

"A minotaur," she said, her long gown swishing around her legs. "Minotaurs are amazing."

"Well, that just leaves us," Paige told me. "Are you done eating?"

At my nod, we stood.

Paige worried her lower lip as we left the room. "I'm not sure if I want to win or not."

Oh, we wanted to win a steamy prize.

I was going to make sure that we did.

PAIGE

We gathered in the foyer, and Monica and Trevor gave each of us matching scarves, hats, and mittens knit from bright red yarn and embroidered with hollies like the ones featured in her wedding.

"You can keep them after," she said gaily. Her cheeks were rosy already, and she kept beaming at Trevor. Happiness for my friend and her new husband soared through me, followed by a touch of longing. What would it be like to be with someone who loved me completely?

"Let me help you, mate," Gunner said, pulling the hat down over Rylee's eyes while she laughed. She did the same thing to him, and when he started tickling her, she squealed. He tossed her over his shoulder again, something she seemed to adore, and strode down the hall to the backside of the castle.

Raze took one look at Elisa holding out a hat to place on his head and snatched it from her grasp. So much for the crush I thought he was developing at breakfast.

With a huff, Elisa pivoted on her heel. She stalked down the hall with him following.

"Let me help you," Darrow said, taking the gifts from me. I'd dressed in a long wool coat, but I'd only brought thin gloves, not anticipating spending much time outside.

He wrapped the scarf around my neck and secured it at my throat, kissing my nose as he finished tying it. The gesture nudged aside some of my envy for my friend's happiness.

He plunked the tasseled hat on my head and tied the silly dangling braids beneath my chin. Holding up the mittens, he grinned. "Would you like me to pin them to your coat?"

Memories of Mom urging us to go play in the snow and securing our mittens to our sleeves so we wouldn't lose them shot through me, wrapping me up in the warmth of being with my old friend. The feeling was shadowed with the sorrow I'd felt when I lost him. Now, I was filled with the joy of having him back in my life.

"Not yet," I said, taking his hat and scarf from him. "I need to help you get ready first." I curled my finger, urging him to lean forward. There was no way I could reach him otherwise. "You grew taller since I last saw you, Darrow."

"One good thing about the curse, I suppose. Remember how puny I was? I didn't think I'd hit five-eight."

"There's nothing wrong with short guys, but I like your new height. What are you now, six-six or so?" I wound the scarf around his neck and secured it, but he was too tall for me to reach his nose for a kiss.

"Six-ten."

"Whoa. I didn't grow much taller after we left town. I'm five-four."

He frowned. "Does our size difference bother you?"

"Only now, when I want to put the hat on your head."

He bent forward until his face was level with mine. "Better?"

So much. "Will your . . . hair mind me touching it?"

"So far, it seems pretty happy whenever you do," he said with a grin.

I laughed, enjoying this time with him. We were only getting dressed to go outside, but this combined old memories with new ones. It felt right.

I carefully tugged the hat onto his head, but it became a challenge when his bands of hair kept coiling around my wrists and fingers, stroking them. It tickled, making me laugh, and he joined in.

"You're making them do that," I said, trying to scowl.

He kissed my nose again. "They act on their own."

Were *they* doing what *he* wanted to do? That tell I was searching for was strutting about before my eyes.

In all honesty, I wouldn't mind a real kiss, not just the teasing advances he kept making that made me want to wrap myself around him and urge him to press me against the wall.

I tugged some more, covering most of his head with the hat. His hair stuck out about six inches below, the tips of the bands weaving in the air. Some people might be frightened by them, but they only made me adore Darrow more.

"Oh, my," Monica said, pointing above us. "Now who would put mistletoe in a place like that?"

"What about this fiend?" Trevor said, holding a small stalk of the bright green leaves over her head. "I believe you need to pay the mistletoe price, lovely mate."

"I'm quite willing, sir," she said, tipping her head back for his kiss.

As I studiously tied the braided bands beneath Darrow's chin, I didn't meet his eye. What if he didn't want to kiss me? I wouldn't push for something I needed more than almost anything.

"Mittens?" I asked, holding them up.

"Let's put them on when we go outside," he said. His finger nudged toward the ceiling. "Do you want a pass on the mistletoe, or are you willing to pay the price?"

"I don't know, Darrow," I said, pretending to frown. My heart danced around in my chest, urging me to get to it. "Do you think the price will be too steep?" Looking up at him, I grinned.

"Why don't we see?" When I continued to grin, he lifted me off my feet and nudged me back against the wall.

I, of course, *had* to wrap my legs around him to make sure I didn't fall.

His head lowered, and for the first time since we were sweet sixteen, he kissed me.

My heart had been sleeping all these years, and it

suddenly awoke in a flurry of emotion. Heat radiated off his body, pulling me deeper into his kiss. His soft lips were supple against mine, gentle yet demanding at the same time. His tongue stroked my lips, begging for entry, and I opened my mouth to let him in.

He tasted like warm cider and cinnamon with just the right amount of heat. His hand stroked my side while the other one supported me with a palm beneath my butt. Being close to him like this reminded me of the way we used to love each other before my parents stole me away.

He groaned, and the sound sunk through me, sparking every nerve ending in my body. My soul came alive, singing in joyous harmony with my heart. I was electrified as he deepened our embrace. His fingers intertwined with mine, and he placed them over my head, bringing back memories of stolen kisses on hot summer days. I moaned as he finally pulled away from me.

His gaze met mine. "Paige."

Rhythmic thuds came closer, and Grannie Vi poked her head up beside us. "Maybe you two won't need to win my little treat after all?"

I snickered, and Darrow's laugh joined in. The moment had broken, but warmth still coursed through me, like I was a pot about to boil over that had been pulled away from the flame. It wouldn't take much to make me simmer once more.

A glance around showed we were alone in the lobby other than Grannie and Uncle Bub. He watched us with a speculative gleam in his eyes.

"Someone stole all the party favors," Grannie Vi said. "Me and Bub are going to the kitchen to ask them to bring a tray up to the ballroom for us."

"Snacks are always welcome," Uncle Bub said with a nod.

Darrow lowered my feet to the floor and took my hand, holding tight, as if he never wanted to let go.

"Let's do it, Elvira," Uncle Bub said, nudging her side.

"You're such a sweet talker, Bub," Grannie said with a snicker. "We can talk about our new matchmaking idea while we're watching them craft snow sculptures."

"Matchmaking idea?" I asked, intrigued.

"Retirement's a hoot until you sit around talking about body parts that don't work as well as they used to," Grannie said. "That's why me and Bub decided to open a matchmaking service."

"We understand love," Bub said, grinning Grannie's way.

"That sounds amazing," I said. "I wish you all the best." Imagine the matches they'd make. What a hoot.

"Do you think any of the couples will create a snow dildo?" Grannie asked Uncle Bub as they caned down the hall, aiming for the kitchen. "*That* would be amazing."

"A snow dildo, huh?" I said, snickering.

"It wouldn't be the first."

I frowned. "Have you made a snow dildo?"

"No, but you'd be surprised by what people want me to create out of stone."

Ha ha. "I need to hear more about this."

"And I'll be happy to share, but the snow's awaiting."

Taking my hand, he rushed me down the hall like we were kids once more. We burst outside.

The castle staff had mounded piles of snow in the backyard, and I assumed we wouldn't truly be carving. This would be more like molding, the way people did when they made a snowman. It wouldn't be anything like the art Darrow created, but the task was going to be fun because I'd get to do it with him.

Overnight, the world had been transformed into a winter wonderland. A thick white carpet had settled over the rolling hills behind the castle, hiding colorful gardens and coating the evergreens like they'd been dusted with confectionary sugar.

Clouds covered the sun, but muted light made shadows dance around us.

The other couples worked on their mounds already, leaving one for us.

"What should we make?" I asked Darrow. Our "palette" was equal to his height and about ten feet across. "I've seen kids do this sort of thing at winter carnivals. They make dragons lying on the ground or sleighs." I waved a mitten-clad hand to the bottles of food coloring sitting on a bench nearby. "We can decorate it with those."

"We should use this," Elisa said with a long-suffering sigh. She and Raze were working on the pile to our left. She held up what looked like a mini chainsaw or one of those electric blades you used to trim the hedges.

Raze grumbled, lifting his big, knobby hands. He'd stuffed his hat on his head and he wore his scarf, but other than black dress pants, he only wore a button-up white shirt and, unbelievably enough, a tie snug at his throat. He wore no coat, but he wasn't shivering. Maybe he had thick skin.

Did he ever dress casually? But then, here he was more than Trevor's cousin enjoying an activity. As a wedding planner, this was also part of his job.

Maybe if he dressed in a flannel shirt and jeans, the casual attire might sink into his yellow skin.

"Really?" he said. "You think we'd be able to precisely carve snow with that?" He rolled his green eyes partly hidden behind his glasses, and if I hadn't been staring, I wouldn't have seen the way his lips subtly twitch upward. Was he teasing her? If so, she wasn't seeing it that way. Leave it to a guy to bumble around trying to attract a woman. "How you're able to come up with artful wedding adornments is beyond me." He hefted a trowel and held it out to her. "Why not use this instead?"

She stared down at it. "That looks like something we'd use to decorate a wedding cake."

"You, perhaps," he said with a lift of his big nose. "I prefer more delicate tools." Again, it looked like he was holding back a smile.

"*You*, delicate?" With a huff, Elisa lowered the maybe-chainsaw to the ground and snatched the trowel from his grip. "Show me, then, Mr. Wonderful Wedding Planner. How am I supposed to use it? I haven't done this before."

"Well, I have, and I'll be delighted to instruct you."

"I'm sure you would."

I ignored their bickering and selected a trowel from the pile of tools near our sculpture. Good point about the tool, Raze. "Why don't we make a bear or a horse?" I asked Darrow.

"I was thinking of . . ." He leaned near and lowered his voice. "A castle."

"Oh! Yes, that sounds perfect."

A hammer in hand, Gunner was beating away at his and Rylee's mound of snow while Rylee cringed, darting here and there to avoid the flying clumps of snow.

She caught my eye and grinned. "I don't believe we're going to win the prize for this event, do you?"

I wasn't discounting Gunner yet. He was clever and diligent.

The scrapes of shovels and other tools rang out as Monica and Trevor worked on a possible snow tree. If they could carve ornaments into the surface, it was going to give us stiff competition. As they worked together diligently, the soothing thrum of their tools filled the air. They worked along to the carols piping from a speaker mounted on the back of the castle.

Rylee laughed again and handed Gunner another tool. He seemed happy to work on the structure all by himself with her supervision.

I turned to find Darrow just as eagerly crafting our sculpture and hurried over to help.

"Tell me what to do," I said. "I want to be a part of this." I'd missed out on doing anything with my friend all these years, and I wasn't going to let any more time slip past us.

"Why don't you work on the moat?" He pointed to where he'd left an unfinished mound stretching out from the front wall of his already impressive structure.

I stepped back to admire what he'd done already, though he'd only worked on the outer walls, leaving a taller mound in the center where we'd construct the pièce de résistance, the castle itself.

Thick stone walls stretched out from the base of the castle, encircling it in a protective embrace. The walls were punctuated by tall turrets with conical roofs, giving it a storybook feel.

Magic surrounded us, warming my heart as I dropped to my knees and started carving a river with ripples and a drawbridge stretching across it.

"Doin' good, babe. Doin' good," Rylee said, grinning at the actually decent-appearing standing bear Gunner was creating. He worked on the sides, making careful gouges to simulate fur. Its ears cocked forward, and it lifted its shout as if scenting the air.

"You have a knack for carving, Gunner," I said. "You're going to give me and Darrow stiff competition."

"I'm afraid *we're* going to lose," Elisa said, coming over to drop to her heels beside me. "Awesome castle, by the way. Our dragon's rather lopsided, though I guess we're giving it a good try."

I peered to where Raze still worked on the dragon. "The contest isn't over yet."

"If we weren't squabbling when we first started, we wouldn't have messed up the tail. It's too short."

"Grab some more snow and fix it."

She nodded slowly. "I guess I could do that."

"And while you're at it, stop squabbling. Maybe grin at him and see what happens."

She shot a speculative gleam toward Raze. "He's such a snooty, stuffy, snobby pain in the ass."

I carefully constructed a railing along one side of my bridge. Master sculptor that he was, Darrow had already made huge progress with our castle. It was going to be amazing when finished. I couldn't wait to start adding color. "Why do you think he's a pain in the ass?"

"Because he is?"

"He irritates you."

She rolled her eyes. "He sure does. I can't understand why Monica hired her own wedding planner when Trevor's cousin, Raze, could run the show by himself. But here I am, trying to make this work as best I can."

"You and Monica are friends. And you've done an amazing job."

"Thanks. I needed this job. I just moved to Monsterville to start over, and things are going to be tight until business picks up."

I peered up at her, squinting through the hazy sunshine. "Maybe I'm seeing it wrong, but when you're not snarling at him, he looks at you with something interesting in his eyes."

"That's irritation," she said. "Everything I say makes him snap."

"Nope, it's heat."

She gasped, blinking at Raze, who continued to work on their dragon. "He can't like me. I . . ."

"You what?"

"If he does, I'm not sure what to do about it." She tapped her chin and cocked her hip. "I mean, I've just moved to Monsterville. He has a wedding planning business that's doing great, though I do believe the town's big enough to support two wedding planners. But if we dated . . ."

"You could combine businesses."

"Oh, hell, no. I'm too independent for that. Can you imagine working with him?"

"He's cute. Why not?"

"Huh." She continued to frown. "He is. Do you think he wears that suit to bed?"

"Why not ask him?"

A grin split her face. "Yeah, right."

This would be fun to watch. I expected their fireworks were going to light up the entire town.

"He's kind of amazing in an ogre way," she said, her head tilting. "Those glasses . . . I want to slide them off his face and stare into his pretty green eyes."

"Why don't you go tell *him* that instead of me?" I said with a low laugh.

"No way. I can't do anything like that. He's my competition. Kissing up to him would . . . I don't know, mess things up."

Maybe they both needed to get messy. This was *really* going to be fun to watch. At least I'd have a ringside show when I returned to Monsterville.

"I guess you've come to an impasse," I said.

She tapped her chin. "I guess I have." Leaving me, she

returned to where Raze was still working. He shot her a scowl, and I shook my head, giggling.

"What?" Darrow asked.

"Just enjoying the fireworks."

He peered around. "I don't see any."

"They're an unusual kind, though they blaze just as bright."

CHAPTER 12

DARROW

"Time's up!" Bart called out.

He trotted up onto the deck behind us and shifted his hooves on the decking beside three other staffers I remembered seeing in the dining room.

Poppy stood proudly beside their impressive minotaur snow sculpture.

Bart shot her a grin before waving a front hoof in our direction. "If you'll kindly step away from your sculptures, our team of staff will study each of them. They've agreed to view our sculptures impartially and will decide which is best to award the prize." He dangled a tall silver bag with a gold bow.

The three clipboard-wielding staffers hurried down the stairs and strode over to us, their gazes fixed on our sculptures.

Bart followed them, trotting over to join Poppy. His arm went around her waist, and I sensed things were getting serious between them. I was happy for them both; everyone deserved happiness.

Monica and Trevor came over to stand with me and Paige.

"Your sculpture is gorgeous," Monica said with a sigh, shooting their train engine a sad smile. She leaned into Trevor's side, and his arm went around her, lifting her up. He plunked her on his shoulder, and she latched onto his left horn. "We did a great job. I love the little guy you carved in the window, sweetheart. He's smiling, and that makes me happy."

"Your wheels are amazing." He turned his head, and she curled forward to kiss him.

Paige grinned my way. "We've created some stiff competition." She held up her palm for a high five.

The staff scribbled on their scoresheets, pausing at each sculpture.

Gunner and Rylee's bear wasn't half bad, and that was saying something considering I was a sculptor.

Raze and Elisa had hacked away at their dragon, but it looked more like a mound of colored snow with a very short, spiked tail. She kept shooting him confused glances from beneath her lashes, and he wore a perpetual scowl. The fireworks Paige mentioned were going to light up the sky.

Moving past our castle, the judges stopped by Raze and Elisa's work. They nodded and whispered before checking out Gunner and Rylee's, and Bart and Poppy's. After, they returned to the back deck.

"If you'll all come inside," one of them called out,

releasing a shiver. "We'll finish tallying our scores and announce the winning team."

"Yes, come along everyone," Bart said, taking Poppy's hand and urging her up onto the deck. "After the prize is awarded, we'll share Monica and Trevor's plans for the afternoon and evening."

"Come on, you two," Monica said with a smile as Trevor strode past us with her still riding on his shoulder. "I want to sip some cocoa in front of the fireplace I saw in the small living room this morning." She leaned close to Trevor and whispered. His low, husky chuckle suggested they might seek out a more private fire for their "cocoa".

"What do you think?" Paige asked, smiling up at me. "Should we get some cocoa and sit in front of the fire too?"

If only our relationship was at a place where I could respond like Trevor, suggest we go make our own fire. Someday? It was my goal.

"Cocoa sounds amazing, as does the fire." I held the door open for her to enter ahead of me, following her inside.

"I love chocolate," she said. "In any way, shape, or form."

"Candy bars?" I asked as we took off our outerwear, handing it to the waiting staff. We heeled off our boots and left them on the rubber mat by the door.

"Oh, definitely."

We started down the hall.

"How about chocolate cake with lots of gooey choco-late frosting?" I asked.

"Yup." She shot a grin over her shoulder, her gaze narrowed on my face. "Where are you going with this, Darrow?"

We reached the foyer and paused.

"Ice cream with hot sauce?" I wiggled my eyebrows, and my hair flared out away from my head, responding to the heat building inside me.

She frowned at it, and when she held her hand near, one of the bands coiled around her finger. It latched onto her like I wanted to do.

"Any kind of chocolate." She tugged her finger away, but instead of backing off, she teased it down the front of my shirt, sliding the tip between two buttons to touch. "Your skin is warm."

"Sadly, I'm not made of hot chocolate."

She shot a flushed look up at me. "That doesn't mean you're not equally edible."

Hell, yeah, I was.

Because I couldn't resist, I whispered by her ear. "Let's find some chocolate sauce, dribble it on each other, then lick it off."

CHAPTER 13

PAIGE

Despite the chilly air swirling around us from the open door, my skin burst into flame.

"I've never done anything like that," I said, picturing myself lying on a soft surface while Darrow dribbled chocolate sauce on my body, then licked it off. I'd do the same thing for him.

"Pity," he said, his gaze trained on my mouth. "I think you'd like it."

I would. No doubt about that.

"Have you?" I gulped out as the rest of our group passed us, heading into the front parlor where a fire crackled merrily.

"Not yet." He took my hand and led me along with them. "I've been waiting for the right time, right place, and right person."

Me?

I knew this guy inside and out, or I had ages ago. His exterior had changed quite a bit, but he was still the

Darrow I believed I was in love with when I was sixteen. I couldn't quite reconcile that skinny friend with the muscular, sexy-talking gorgon standing beside me.

One thing was clear: he wanted me any way I was willing to give myself to him. It was up to me to decide what and when. I sensed he wouldn't push for anything I didn't want to give, but if I told him to take me to bed right now, he would.

And I'd enjoy it, chocolate sauce or not. I knew that deep within my bones.

"Inside here," the staff member said ahead of us, directing us into the room. As if Monica had called ahead to place her order, mugs of steaming cocoa sat on a table near the fire.

"Grab a cup," Bart said. "Sit by the fire and warm up a bit. The judges are tallying the scores, and they'll make the announcement soon." His tails swished back and forth behind him, long and thin with a bushy tip—the color matching the long mane surrounding his face.

Poppy grabbed a cup, squirted whipped cream on top, and sidled over to sit with him on the sofa. When she licked the cream, his eyes widened, but he grinned and whispered something that made her skin darken.

They made a cute couple, and I wished them all the best.

Darrow handed me a mug, and when he sat beside me near the fire, leaning close, one of his hair tips stroked my cheek.

"They like me," I said, lifting my mug to take a sip. As the cocoa touched my lips, a feeling of warmth radiated across my skin. The smooth texture glided down my throat, coating it with heat, though it couldn't compare to the fire licking through me from Darrow's touch. Did I dare suggest we sneak away and see what we could do with a can of whipped cream?

"*Every* part of me likes you, Paige, not just my hair," he said. His gaze remained locked on mine as he drank. When he lowered the cup, his tongue dipped out to lick off a bit of chocolate on his upper lip, and I pictured that tongue gliding across my nipples. Other intimate areas too.

I met his gaze. "What do you plan to do about—"

"We have a winner," Bart called out, his hooves clicking on the hardwood floor as he stood. He trotted over to stand among us. "First, let me tell you that our judges had a very difficult time deciding, and all the scores were quite high. In fact, they had to re-tally the numbers more than once before they could confirm the winner. Our sculptures are so amazing, they'll be show-cased by the castle over the next few weeks." His gaze swept through the room, taking in each of us, finishing on Poppy. He gave her a wink.

Monica sat on the sofa on Trevor's lap, encircled in his embrace. She'd tipped her head back to look up at Trevor, and I suspected she was more interested in where she could lounge in front of a fire naked than in hearing who won.

Gunner held Rylee in a similar manner, though they'd taken an oversized squishy chair near the window.

"Wait for us," Grannie Vi called out. "Don't announce anything yet!" She and Uncle Bub entered the room, their canes clunking on the floor in harmony, and settled on a big squishy sofa together. She lifted her cane, pointing the tip at the room in general. "You may now proceed."

Uncle Bub grinned. "Mighty amazin' sculptures out there. My bones would be frozen, but you young folks have plenty of vigor left inside you."

Grannie whispered something that made his wrinkly cheeks go pink, and he chuckled, slapping her thigh.

"I have a feeling they'll park our bear somewhere near the woods," Rylee said with a merry laugh. "Or maybe we can take it home and put it on our front lawn." She giggled when Gunner nuzzled her neck, whispering something that made her arms tighten around him.

Even Raze and Elisa leaned forward in excitement, though they'd chosen two upright chairs with a coffee table between them. She shot him a look I couldn't define. Longing? Nah, she didn't like him. She'd made it clear he was about to become her stiffest competition, that she was going to do anything to make sure her business succeeded despite his potential interference.

Raze was an unknown to me. I'd seen him around town a few times, but we'd never talked. From a distance, I'd caught his uptight expression, and since he perpetually wore a business suit, I got the feeling he wouldn't be much fun at a party. But my mother always said that still waters run deep.

"It's clear to us who won," Grannie Vi shouted.

"Please," Bart said, holding up a front hoof. "Each sculpture is equally stunning in its own way."

"That's what I was sayin'," Uncle Bub said. "That bear darn near makes my bones shiver." He wiggled in his seat. "And the dragon? I kept expectin' it to shoot flames."

Elisa grinned at Raze, who was looking Uncle Bub's way, and missed it.

"As for the castle, I'd be tempted to set up housekeeping there if I didn't have a fine suite at Violet's B&B. Besides, she needs me to make my special scone recipe each Sunday."

Grannie Vi shot him a denture-filled smile and patted his arm. "Your scones *are* amazing, Bub."

"And as for the train engine, I haven't seen such fine workmanship in ages," he added. "And you and Poppy's minotaur looks like he could be your brother."

Poppy grinned. "We did a great job."

"Exactly," Bub said.

"See?" Gunner said to Rylee. "I told you it was perfect."

"*You're* perfect," she said. His head swooped down, and he gave her a lingering kiss.

"Now you know why the judges had such a hard time making their decision," Bart said. "But there can only be one pair of winners and . . ." He fluttered a piece of paper in the air. "It's Darrow and Princess Paige!"

"Princess?" Monica giggled and slapped a hand over her mouth as the other staff members beamed my way.

CHAPTER 14

DARROW

I rose to my feet and bowed deeply to Paige, taking her hand. I kissed it, grinning up at her.

"We need to tell them I'm not a princess," she whispered.

"Nah, let them think they're entertaining royalty. It'll give them something to brag about later."

Her conspiratorial grin sunk through my bones. Definitely needed to get her alone with some chocolate syrup.

"If one of you will come over," Bart said. "I'll give you the prize." He waved a hoof to the tall silver bag sitting on a nearby table.

I strode over and grabbed the bag, peeking inside while I walked back to Paige. I sank down beside her and shot her a mischievous smile. "You won't believe what's in here."

"What's in there?" she asked.

I tugged out a bottle of bubble bath and a sponge on a wooden stick.

"Oh, that must be from Grannie Vi," Paige said with a giggle. "Thank you, Grannie Vi!"

"They're not from her," I whispered.

"Actually, they're from us," Monica said. "It's a gag gift, though you're welcome to use it any way you'd like. There are bathtubs in all the bedrooms."

I'd already noted the big claw-footed tub sitting near my windows. Paige's room had one as well?

"I have some ideas for that bubble bath," Paige said, taking the sponge from my hands. She winked my way and lowered her voice. "If someone could locate some chocolate, we might be able to have a party." She nudged her chin to the tray that had held the mugs of cocoa, where a brown bottle of syrup sat. "I have a few ideas for that."

"Actually," I said softly. "Grannie Vi's prize is still in the bag. Are you open to giving me carte blanche with the prize and the chocolate?"

CHAPTER 15

PAIGE

I wasn't sure where our teasing was taking us, but I couldn't wait to find out.

We drank our cocoa. Before I could suggest I might actually want to take a long soak in a tub, Bart called out again.

"Lunch is being served in the dining room, and after that, we have a lovely surprise for you all."

Monica clapped her hands in excitement. Trevor beamed, and I could tell he must be involved in the planning.

"Right this way, Princess," one of the staff members called out, waving my way. "The bride and groom should enter first, but as royalty, you must go second."

"I'm not a princess," I whispered as I passed her, leaving the parlor through the door connecting this room to the next.

"Flying under the radar, are we, Your Highness?" she asked with a wink. "I understand. If I was royal, I'd worry about the paparazzi too. Rest assured; your secret is safe with us. No one will say a word to the press."

"Ah, um." I pinched my eyes shut and grabbed Darrow's hand, tugging him behind me into the dining room. I leaned against his arm as we rounded the big dining room table to find our seats. "You're in trouble, big boy."

He reeled back, but grinned. "Me?"

"Yes, you," I hissed. "You've convinced the staff I'm a hidden princess."

"There's nothing like living the life of a royal." He held out my chair for me to sit.

"But I'm not," I said over my shoulder as I slid into my seat.

"To me, you are." He helped nudge me forward, then snatched up my napkin that had been folded into a three-dimensional swan and draped it across my lap. "For you, Your Royal Highness, I only want the best."

That was him. I knew it for sure.

"As long as we convince them before we leave," I said, relenting.

"We can do that."

He dropped into the chair beside me while our friends settled around us. Grannie Vi and Uncle Bub hobbled into the room complaining about aching backs and hips and dropped into the chairs on Darrow's right.

Grannie leaned around Darrow, peering my way. "Did someone call you princess?"

"It's a cutesy name," I said. "It doesn't mean anything."

"Fake it until you make it, I always say." She gave me a sassy nod. "Haven't you heard of visualization? If you truly believe something will happen, it's bound to come true. I did that once with the lottery."

"You won the lottery?" I asked, stunned.

"Well, only a few scratch tickets. But one of them won me ten dollars." She tapped her temple. "I visualized it, and it came true." Leaning back, she nudged Bub's side. "What do you think, sweetheart?"

"That I'm hungry and that the gosh-darn staff better bring out the food pronto," he grumbled.

She grunted. "I hope they serve beans."

"Why beans?" Darrow asked, probably to make conversation. Why else ask?

Grannie Vi leaned close to him, lowering her voice to her version of a whisper, which, for the rest of us, came out at a medium screech. "They keep me regular."

"Ah, I see," Darrow said. "That's important."

"Darn right it is," Uncle Bub said. "Wait until you're our age. You kids think things get easier as you get older, 'cause we're retired and all, but I'm here to tell you, nuthin' gets easier. You worry about your joints failin' you at the worst times—"

"Like during sex," Grannie Vi jumped in to say.

Rylee groaned. Cringing, she pressed her face into Gunner's chest. He was soaking up every word Grannie said like she was an oracle come down from the heavens to predict which stocks would surge on the market.

"Tell it, Grannie," Bub said. "These youngins just don't realize how good they have it. Why, when I was your age, I didn't get married in a castle like this." He leaned close to Grannie. "Please pardon me for speaking about her."

"I understand, dear," she said, patting his arm resting on the table. "She was a part of your life, and I'm sure you're better because you knew her."

He huffed. "That's debatable. Divorced her after I caught her in bed with our neighbor. But as I was sayin', after we got married at a regular old church, we hopped in my jalopy and headed to the city for a few nights. None of this fancy stuff for us."

"It was like that for me and my dearly departed husband," Grannie said, peering up at the heavens. "Rest his soul. We had a simple ceremony and a simple honeymoon."

We were saved from further enlightening conversation when the staff brought out covered dishes with a variety of food, enough to satisfy eight hungry sculptors and two elderly relatives.

"Here you are, Your Highness," someone said from behind me. "We thought you might enjoy a dish more worthy of your lofty status." She placed a plate in front of me.

I stared down at a pile of round seashells about the size of my thumb, floating in butter.

"Ah, thank you," I said.

"Escargot," Grannie exclaimed. She scowled at the steak tips revealed on one of the platters, the buttered potatoes, and the mix of vegetables accompanying the meal. "I don't suppose . . ." She extended her fork my way.

Thankfully, after delivering my dish, the staff scurried back to the kitchen, perhaps to hunt down a wild boar to serve for my second course.

I lifted the entire plate and handed it to Grannie. "I don't see any beans, sadly, but you can have these as a consolation prize."

"Ah, never worry about that, love. I'll take some fiber supplements before I go to sleep tonight."

After that, we dished up the food and ate.

Rylee and Trevor were quite good at handling their elderly relative. Grannie tried to drive the conversation into bedroom activities at least three times, but Rylee distracted her by asking her to tell us stories from when she was little. Trevor suggested she sing, which maybe wasn't such a great idea when Uncle Bub joined in, sloshing his cup of beer back and forth.

The sweet old lady shared what it was like growing up on the coast of Massachusetts with eight siblings, keeping us all chuckling about their antics.

When she started to lag and brought up the merits of alien dildos, I steered the conversation to speculation about what the afternoon surprise might be.

"We're going sledding," Darrow said with complete certainty.

"There aren't any big hills near the castle," I said.

"Sure there are," Bart said. He's taken a seat with Poppy at everyone's urging. "The hill out front would do nicely." He winked at Monica, who giggled.

Okay, so sledding might be in our future.

"Actually . . ." I said. "I think the afternoon's made for a bubble bath."

"Oh, hell, yeah," Monica said with a grin. "I double bought the sponge on a stick, so a bath is on my agenda for sure."

"I'll be happy to wash your back," Trevor said.

She tickled his side, and his rough laughter burst out. "And I'll be happy to let you."

"What about you, Paige?" Darrow asked softly.

I grinned and lowered my voice. "I think that scrub brush has your name on it."

CHAPTER 16

DARROW

I was going to climb into the bath with Paige, not just scrub her back. And I had some ideas about other areas I could scrub while I was at it.

My cock was on fire, threatening to burst into a full erection whenever Paige teased me like that. Payback was going to be extra sweet.

Chocolatey, in fact.

Heat buzzed through my veins, but I took a strange satisfaction in telling my body to slow down and wait. When Paige and I finally came together—and hell, yeah, we would—I wanted her in as high a fever pitch as me.

My goal was to have her writhing, pretty much begging, before I swept her up and laid her on a bed.

They brought out plates of tiny cakes after the meal, and we ate until we felt we were going to burst.

Bart rose and moved around to the head of the table, his fanged grin taking us all in. "I see you've enjoyed your meals." His gaze went from the plate of empty snail shells I'd wisely taken back from Grannie Vi after she ate them, to me, and his grin widened. "Are we ready for our late-afternoon activity?"

"Yes," Monica exclaimed, clapping.

Who would've thought an after-a-wedding weekend could be this fun? I thought I'd be bored, that I'd be making excuses to Trevor to leave early. Instead, I wanted to remain in this magical place forever.

"Raze told me what we're doing next," Elisa said, shooting him a shy smile that he seemed oblivious to. Did he notice she'd gone from snarling at him to crushing? Maybe not. I didn't know Raze well, but from what I'd seen, he was highly focused on building his business and completely unaware of anything else.

She was sweet, though, and I could see how they might fit together nicely. Why should two wedding planners compete when they could work together to make one well-running machine? Maybe they'd end up giving a combined effort a try. Then, they'd be a powerhouse wedding planning business.

"If you'll all bundle up for an outdoor activity and join us out front," Bart said. "We're going for sleigh rides!"

"Oh, that sounds romantic," Elisa said. She peeked up at Raze through her lashes.

Raze had his phone out, and I assumed he'd organized this event and was checking "sleigh rides" off on his list. If any other activities or treats were included in the event, he'd speak with Bart to ensure they were presented at the perfect time and place as well.

"Let's go, everyone," Monica said, her smile taking all of us in as she rose from her chair.

"Not me," Uncle Bub said. "I'm not freezin' my ass off outside when I could sit in front of the fire and sip some wine." He glanced at Grannie Vi. "What do you say, Elvira? Join them and risk patootie frostbite or cozy up to me near the fire?"

"Wine and a fire, you say? Why Bub." She grinned and tapped his arm. Rising to her feet, she grabbed her cane she'd leaned against the table. "You're not planning on getting me tipsy and seducing me, are you?"

"Would you like me to?" he asked, his face scrunching. He also got up and took his cane, following her toward the door.

She giggled and picked up her pace, clunking out into the hall. "Why don't you follow me and find out?"

"Women," Uncle Bub said to us all. "I always felt a man was given one choice in life when it came to 'em. You can love 'em, or you can understand 'em. It's a toss-up for me right now, but maybe now's the time to find out. I'll see you youngin's later—much later."

With that, he left the room.

Monica snickered behind her fingers.

Trevor rolled his eyes. "Too much information for me."

"For sure." Rylee took Gunner's hand. "What do you think? Loving or understanding?"

"Both," he said. "I'm picking both."

"He's a wise orc," Paige said, joining me as we left the room.

We dressed for the cold and met out front on the walkway.

Across the drive, a dual metal track cut through the snow, arcing around the inside of the driveway. A horse's neigh rang out from our left, and a sleigh pulled by two fake horses glided in our direction, followed by four more vehicles.

"There's mulled wine in a flask by your feet, plus mugs," Bart said from beside us. He'd placed a bright green hat on his head—his horns jutting up from each side, plus a matching coat with fuzzy white trim. He wore no boots, but I assumed he had equal traction with his hooves on wood and carpet. "Warmed blankets await you for your leisurely ride through the forest. The ride takes about an hour, and when you return, we'll bustle you inside to join your elderly relatives by the fire."

I was eager for the ride; less eager to join Vi and Bub by the fire if we were going to interrupt something I'd have to bleach my eyes out after seeing.

CHAPTER 17

PAIGE

Me and Darrow climbed into the last sleigh and settled on the cushioned seat. One of our two fake horses shook its head, rattling the reins, and the other released a snicker.

"Amazing," I said, completely enchanted.

Darrow covered us with the toasty warm blankets, tucking them up around my neck, leaning forward to kiss me on my nose. "Warm enough?"

"Yup." I'd been simmering since our teasing about chocolate. Would he act on it soon?

"Wine?" he asked, lifting the flask and mugs.

I nodded, and he poured each of us a cup. The heady scent of cinnamon and cloves drifted through the air, and when I took a sip, the flavors glided across my tongue.

The sleigh hitched forward, the fake horses' legs shifting back and forth as if they pulled us across the front lawn.

I snuggled against Darrow, my heart racing as his warmth engulfed me.

The horses pulled us across the driveway and into the snow-covered woods, the crunch of the crisp white powder beneath the runners echoing in the silent night.

A thick blanket of snow covered everything around us, creating a magical winter wonderland. Icicles hung from each branch, glimmering in the light of the setting sun.

As the sun slipped away and the moon rose, the night darkened. Stars shone brightly, adding to the enchantment of the scene. We sat in silence, sipping our mulled wine, but it was a comfortable lull. I could feel our connection, the intensity of it growing with each passing moment.

The horses took us further into the woods. Monica started singing softly ahead of us, the sound of her voice carrying through the stillness of the night. Darrow and I joined in, me humming while his rich baritone echoed in the woods.

His arm slipped around my shoulders, and as his thick bands of hair stroked my nape, I leaned into him. There couldn't be a more special moment. As we continued our journey, I knew that no matter what happened in our future, I would remember this night and the feeling of being wrapped up in his arms, surrounded by the beauty of nature.

The sleighs spaced out, putting us far enough apart that we couldn't hear anyone else speaking. I assume they did this to add to the magical experience, giving us the feeling we were alone in the woods with no one else around.

I finished my wine, its warmth sinking through me, making my skin pulse and my bones go melty.

I leaned into Darrow's embrace, snug and toasty with him beneath the blanket.

"Thirty minutes or so left," he said. "How should we pass the time?'

He said it in a neutral tone, but my mind immediately took me in a sexier direction. Singing was fun, but I had a feeling we could enhance our sleigh ride experience.

"Want to make out?" I asked. "We did that when we rode the Ferris wheel long ago at the Breezewater Fair." Back then, I was a teenage virgin, unaware of what the fluttering in my belly meant.

"I want to kiss you every second of the day." He turned to face me, stroking my chilly cheeks. I leaned into his warm hand. "You were pretty back then, but you're even prettier now."

Anticipation hummed through my veins. I couldn't stop thinking of being close to him.

"There isn't anything I want to do more than strip everything off your body so I can touch and taste you," he said in a husky voice. "But it's awfully cold outside."

"You'll warm me up." Until I exploded. "You do have a point, though. Neither of us wants to be the one with an ass hanging out in the wind."

His low laugh rang out. "There are options. Let me

see what I can do for you, sweet." He tugged me onto his lap, my legs spread on either side of his thighs.

Snowflakes fell around us, coating my silver sort-of boyfriend with confectionary sugar. They dusted his shoulders and even landed on his nose.

The hoot of an owl rang out, echoing in the stillness that only came when snow fell, as if the flakes amplified all sounds. Leafless tree branches creaked and clacked as they shifted in the light wind.

We were alone in a winter wonderland and there was no one else I wanted to be with but Darrow.

He cupped my nape with a warm hand and tugged my mouth close to his. His lips captured mine, and memories of our first kiss and our last flashed through my mind. We thought we were so grown up back then, so able to handle whatever life threw our way.

I hated that we'd missed so much, but I was grateful we were old enough to savor what we were building once more.

While his tongue teased across mine, his warm hands slipped beneath my shirt.

The chill air gave way to a delicious warmth as his fingertips brushed against my belly. A shudder of pleasure ripped through me, and I leaned into his touch.

My breathing came faster as his fingers worked their way up and down my sides, tantalizing each sensitive spot. I wanted more, so much more, and he seemed to know it.

My skin was on fire from his touch, my body alive and pulsing. I craved this moment with a hunger I hadn't felt since the last time we were together. Back then, our simple touch was innocent, though heated. We hadn't realized what we had or what we needed. Would we have reached that point given time?

I liked to think so.

His fingers slid away, moving around to my back to undo my bra. He tugged up my sweater, and the icy breeze made my nipples harden. I should be shivering from the cold, but an inferno blazed inside me, coursing through my veins.

I wrenched off my coat and sweater, dropping them onto the seat beside him along with my hat, scarf, and mittens.

As he tugged the blanket up behind me, draping it over my shoulders, he trailed kisses down my neck, nuzzling my newly exposed skin. His hands gently caressed each breast while his mouth sucked hungrily at one nipple and then the other, sending currents of pleasure radiating throughout my body.

Desire flushed through me, overheating me as he licked and sucked. His fingers moved from my breasts, warming across my back before returning to the front. They slid along my belly before coming to rest on the button of my jeans. Releasing a low cry of need to the night, I pressed myself tightly against him, grinding my groin against the bulge in his pants.

I groped his chest, yanking up his shirt, needing the connection of my palms on his silver skin.

He pressed me against him, making sure I felt the hard bulge in his pants rubbing right where I wanted it most. With a gasp of pleasure, I rocked against him, reveling in the sensation of being so close to him after all the years apart.

His mouth moved to mine, kissing me deeply until I clung to his shoulders, trembling. He lightly traced kisses across my jawline before nuzzling his way over to one of my nipples, sucking hungrily. The exquisite sensation sent waves of excitement through me.

"Pants?" he whispered, his fingers on the top button.

At my nod, he undid the fastener and lowered the zipper. I wrenched to my feet and wrangled out of them, tossing them aside. I couldn't believe how wanton I was behaving, how much I craved him.

With a growl, he tugged me back down on his lap, spreading me wide around him.

"You're dressed," I cried, clawing at his shirt and pants in frustration. "I need skin."

"Soon, love. Now is all about your pleasure." He reached into his pocket and pulled out something, but I couldn't tell what it was in the dark.

As the horses plodded along, their fake hooves thumping on the snowy ground, carrying us along the woodland trail, Darrow stroked my thighs. The patterns he created grew tighter, slowly edging toward my core.

He sucked in one of my nipples just as his finger reached my clit. Something buzzed and vibrated at my core.

I jerked toward him, not caring what it was, riding it like I craved to impale myself on Darrow and ride *him*.

While his tongue stroked across my breast, his finger

hummed. He glided his hand lower, teasing across my opening and dipping back out to rub my clit.

Completely undone, I bucked and rocked, trying to force his fingers inside me.

"Do you want this?" he asked, dipping his vibrating finger inside only long enough to make me crave more. "Or this?" Two fingers slipped all the way to my core before wrenching back out again. "Scream for me."

"Jeez, the others will hear." I could only come up with a rational thought for one second.

"I'm not distracting you enough, am I?"

His gaze locked on mine, and he pumped what felt like three fingers inside me, driving them in deep and pulling them back out to rub against my clit.

We settled into a rocking motion, me pushing forward as he impaled me and me twisting my hips backward as he pulled back out. Each time, he ran his vibrating finger over my clit.

I clung to his shoulders and pounded against him, taking everything he had to give while begging for more.

My body trembled. Damn, I was close. I could feel the tension building to a roaring blaze deep within my core. I slid close to the edge. An intense wave of ecstasy washed over me, and I gasped, pushing myself further. I kept rising toward the peak–begging for it–and it would recede before I could claim it.

"Scream," Darrow whispered in my ear. "Come from my touch. I want to feel it. Hear it. Later, I'm going to taste your come on my tongue. And then I'm going to fuck you hard against the wall. After that, I'll carry you to bed and do it all over again, pushing you to your limit and beyond until you can't think of anything and anyone but me."

I should be shoving away his possessive talk, but my heart and soul drank it in, craving it.

"Take your pleasure from my hand now, love," he said, bending over to suck on my nipple. He released it with a wet smack and greedily went for the other. "Take it."

He rolled my nipple with his teeth, though not hard enough to sting, and tingles shot to my core. I was driven to the crest once more, shaking and keening as I rode his fingers. I thrust my chest out to his mouth.

Like a dam hit with a spring surge after a heavy rain, I gave way, my body quivering and my breath jerking out. The rush of this moment coursed through me, claimed me. I was powerless in the face of such intensity. Powerless as Darrow played my body like a finely strung instrument. I shrieked when it hit me, consumed me, and the sensations kept coming. Wave after wave of pleasure blasted through me, leaving me euphoric and spent.

"Yes," he hissed in my ear. "Like that."

I collapsed against him, caught in his arms, and he enfolded me in the blanket and his touch. He murmured against my hair, but I was so lost in him, I could barely make out what he said.

Finally, after what felt like hours, my body relaxed as the orgasm faded away. His fingers slid out of me, and he held up his hand.

"I do believe I'm enjoying this prize." His grin shone with complete satisfaction despite his engorged cock still pressing against the front of his pants. "Who would've thought a vibrating finger could be as much fun as chocolate?"

CHAPTER 18
DARROW

By the time our sleigh stopped in front of the castle again, I'd helped Paige dress and pictured ice cubes to make my cock settle. It still simmered, but my cock could wait. Making sure Paige was satisfied had been enough.

The others climbed out of their sleighs, and when I caught Trevor carrying Monica into the castle followed by Gunner with Rylee, I suspected we weren't the only ones who'd gotten more out of this than just a ride through the forest.

Elisa stalked ahead of Raze, telling me some of us hadn't. Would they compete with each other with anger or turn it into a game they both could win? There was heat between them, so it could go either way.

Since I was romantic at heart, I hoped they'd find a way to turn this into something amazing.

Holding Paige's hand, we walked up the steps and inside the castle, handing over our winter clothing to the staff and removing our boots, placing them on rubber mats.

I trailed my fingers along her nape, and she shivered, shooting me a shy smile.

"I'm going to take a bath," she said softly.

I leaned in close to whisper by her ear. "Would you like company?"

"I believe so. It seems you keep making promises you've yet to fulfill," she said with a sly smile. "Perhaps it's time you paid up?"

"Go," I said, tapping her ass, urging her toward the stairs. "I won't be far behind."

Heat simmered inside me. There were so many things I wanted to do with her delectable body. Where to start?

She climbed the stairs, pausing on the landing to look down and meet my eye. When she'd left my view, I hurried into the parlor. Spying the bottle of chocolate sauce still sitting on the platter, I snatched it up and tucked it inside my shirt.

"Ah, there you are," one of the staff said, entering the room with a small tray holding a silver covered dish, a bottle, and a snifter glass. "I was looking for the princess. The chef sends her regards and hoped this small offering will make her happy." She studied the bulge in my shirt with a frown before shaking her head. "Shall I bring it up to her?"

And walk in on Paige reclining in her bath? Nope, that was something I planned to do.

"Allow me?" I said, taking the tray from her resisting

fingers. "The princess told me she wanted to rest. I don't believe she'll welcome anyone disturbing her. But I'll take this to her and see if she'd enjoy a treat before sleeping."

"Very well, sir," the woman said, though her frown remained. "I did so hope to reveal the treats to her."

"I'll tell her . . . What is your name?"

"Oh, it's Betty." She dipped into a curtsy. "Betty Partridge."

"I'll tell her they come especially from you, Betty."

Betty's face reddened. "And from the chef."

"Of course. From you, Betty, and the chef."

"Thank you." She dipped forward again in another curtsy before pivoting and rushing from the room.

I peeked under the silver cover, grinning at the big bowl of ice cream. Ha. And they'd included a fine coffee brandy to sip along with it.

I'd deliver it immediately. We couldn't let all the ice cream to melt, now could we? Not unless it melted as it slid down her body.

With a jaunty step, I strode from the parlor and up the stairs. I didn't stop until I'd reached her room. Had I given her enough time to get ready? Or would she stand inside fully dressed and tell me to get lost when I knocked on her door?

I didn't like that the doubts that plagued me for so long have come home to roost in my heart once more. She hadn't chosen to leave me; she was taken. Lied to. Denied the chance to make up her own mind. However, it was hard to rationalize feelings.

Standing outside her door, I was almost tempted to turn and walk in the other direction.

That's when I realized what I was doing to myself. Her parents rejected me, coming by my house to stare in horror at what I'd done. For months, I had no idea how to control the changes within my body. Even now, I sometimes could barely control the urge churning inside me.

But I'd worked hard to overcome this, studying ancient texts and reading online in private monster forums. Finally, I was at a place where I could almost turn a curse into a blessing.

Only my dad, the poor guy who died last year in an accident, had believed in my goodness from the start. Without him, I would've been lost, because I'd already lost Paige.

I wasn't that Darrow any longer. I was Paige's equal once more.

And I loved her, always had, and I would until my dying day.

So, despite my churning emotions trying to send my confidence into a full nosedive, I placed the tray on a nearby table, straightened my clothing, and knocked on her door, murmuring her name.

It creaked open at my touch.

As I grabbed the tray, she called out from inside.

"Come on in, Darrow. The water feels amazing."

CHAPTER 19

PAIGE

I tipped my head back against the side of the giant clawed tub placed in front of a big window overlooking the winter fairytale scene behind the castle. Warm water swirled around me, soothing my bones.

The world outside barely existed.

I still craved Darrow. The fiery orgasm he gave me in the sleigh had sparked a hunger inside me only he could satisfy.

When I reached the room, I filled the tub as fast as the hot water would gush out of the spigot. I worried I wouldn't have the scene set before he arrived.

I drew down the blankets on my big bed, draping them artfully, then snatched a flower from a nearby vase, wiped off the water, and laid it on a pillow. Finding candles in the closet, I placed them strategically around the room and lit them.

Happy with how everything looked, I stripped,

donning only the fluffy white robe provided by the castle.

Anticipation coursed through my veins. One touch, and he was going to light me aflame once more. This time, I was going to be the one making demands. I'd rip off his clothing and show him . . . Well, I wasn't sure what. I'd never wanted anyone like this before.

As the water rose within the tub, I added some bubble bath, savoring the piney, floral scent drifting through the air.

Bubbles steamed and bobbed in the dim light, glistening like oil slicks. I smiled as I remembered him mentioning washing my back. A quick glance revealed the sponge on a stick lying on a chair near the door. I swooped over, snatched it up, and laid it artfully on a low table beside the tub.

"Okay, Darrow. Any time now." I whispered.

He didn't arrive, but I held onto my confidence. I might've been temporarily satisfied in the forest, but he'd had a raging hard-on until we returned to the castle. I imagined it was all he could do to walk.

Maybe I should get into the tub?

Ditching the robe—no, draping it carefully over a chair near the tub—I shut off the water and stepped into the heated goodness.

I leaned back against one end, seeing he'd easily fit on the other. I pictured his legs nestling beside mine.

When he knocked, my breath caught in my throat. He called out, and the door creaked open.

Closing my eyes, I invited him in.

The soft pad of his footsteps was followed by a click as he closed and locked the door.

We were alone together for what I hoped would be the first day of the rest of our lives.

I cracked my eyes open.

Candles flickered in their holders, adding to the hazy, dream-like quality of the moment. The walls threw flickering shadows, making them dance like ghosts. The scent of the candles was calming and sensual, but at the same time, reminding me that life was fleeting. You had to grab onto what was offered and hold tight or it could be stolen.

Look what happened to him, stolen by a fiend who hurt him. It crushed me to think of how scared he must've been. I wasn't sure he'd ever want to talk about that time, and I wouldn't push. If he needed to share, he would. I sensed he'd blocked it out and moved on, which could be the healthiest way for him to deal with it.

"Shall I bathe you, Princess?" he asked in a husky voice. Without waiting for my reply, he leaned down behind me, taking the sponge and dipping it into the water. He lathered up the tip. "Lean forward."

I shivered slightly as he slowly ran the sponge across my shoulders, spreading suds over my skin and moving down toward my bottom. He tossed the sponge aside with a grunt and replaced it with his firm but gentle hands. I closed my eyes, melting from his touch.

His hands moved down in a circular motion against my muscles, and every bit of tension released from my body, turning me as soft as butter. My heart beat loudly in my ears, and I could feel how badly I longed for him.

As if he sensed what I was feeling, he leaned forward to brush my hair away from my neck before raining kisses along my damp nape and shoulders.

My breath caught in my throat as his lips moved down further, trailing across my upper arm. Lifting my arm from the water, he kissed all the way to my fingers. He glided his lips back up to my shoulder and across to give my other arm equal attention. My limbs liquified, and I fell into this moment of pure bliss.

He slowly massaged my arms, paying close attention to each crease and curve. His touch was so gentle I could feel his heart beating through his fingertips in tandem with my own.

I turned towards him, and he paused, meeting my gaze with a tenderness that stole away the last of my doubts. With his hands still dripping with suds, he leaned forward and touched my forehead lightly before trailing his fingertips across my cheeks and down to the curve of my chin.

He kissed me then; one filled with such emotion that it made my heart sing. I almost forgot where we were. My eyes slid closed, and I focused purely on the sensation of his mouth pressing down on mine, his tongue stroking past my lips with a tenderness that brought tears to my eyes. His wet hands held my face while our mouths worked together in perfect harmony. The sensation electrified me, making me feel alive like never before.

Easing back, he grinned and shook his finger my way. "None of that yet. I haven't finished washing your body."

A current surged through me, shooting to my fingers and toes and coiling in my core where I ached for his touch.

He eased around behind me.

"Lean back again," he said, helping me relax against the wall of the tub. Taking a cloth, he ran it gently around my breasts, teasing it up across my nipples until they'd formed rosy, aching buds.

"You're igniting me, Darrow," I whispered.

"Do you know what this is doing to me?"

I glanced down, noting the big bulge in his pants. Water had splashed on the fabric, and it clung to his cock, outlining the long length and thickness.

I salivated at the thought of him plunging it inside me and riding my body until we both fell apart.

After lathering up the cloth again, he leaned over my shoulder and focused on my belly, creating intricate circles on my skin and dipping the cloth down into the water and between my legs. I gasped in pleasure as he gently caressed me, rubbing my clit before gliding the fabric along my opening. His hands never wavered as he explored each sensitive inch of my skin, taking his time to memorize every curve and crevice before moving on.

He left me wanting, moving around to the foot of the tub, where he got the cloth soapy again and began with my feet, lifting one, then the other, out of the water and washing them gently. My calves got equal attention. My thighs. As he slid the cloth down between them, he nudged against my clit, keeping my flame burning brightly.

His touch was both tender and passionate at the same time, making me tremble and wonder what his next move would be.

A current ran through me, building with every stroke of his hand. It seemed like he knew exactly the right pressure to apply to elicit the maximum pleasure from me. I melted against the back of the tub as he worked his magic, pushing all thoughts from my mind except for him.

He dropped the cloth with a wet splat and straightened, wrenching his sweatshirt over his head. Tossing it aside, he ripped off his t-shirt, revealing rippling rows of silver muscles. His pecs were to die for, as were his shoulders that tapered to a narrow waist hugged by his low-slung jeans.

With his gaze locked on mine, he undid the top fastening, then slowly lowered the zipper.

After heeling off his shoes, he tugged down his pants, shifting them aside, and straightened.

His cock was as silver as the rest of him, and hewn to perfection, like the ancient gods had dropped down to earth and crafted him from the rarest steel.

I licked my lips, and he groaned. His cock surged against his abs, long and thick and covered with beads the size of my pinky nail. They shimmered, vibrated.

The head was thicker than the rest, and no matter how much I dreamed about what it might feel like, I sensed it was going to be so much better.

He stepped into the tub, sinking down across from me, and nudged his feet next to my thighs.

Leaning forward, he kissed me again, and I drank in the wonder of his mouth.

His hands slid up to my neck and down the length of my arms until his fingers tangled in mine. He pulled me closer, our chests touching as he brought our mouths together harder and with growing urgency. His soft lips coaxed mine apart so that I could feel the warmth of his tongue on my own.

He broke away again, and this time he watched me as his hands moved lower across my back, skimming over each curve before tracing circles around my sides and up to cup my breasts. He massaged them lightly, taking his time to tease each part of me into a state of complete arousal.

When he eased forward to capture one nipple between his lips, I gasped. He used gentle flicks before circling it with his tongue and drawing on it until it was taut and throbbing in anticipation.

Then he did the same with the other nipple before kissing me again, tugging me up onto his lap with me straddling him. This time I felt more than just his mouth; I felt all of him as he pressed his length against me.

His hands continued south, stroking over the swell of my belly before moving between my legs. I groaned as his fingers slipped inside me, sending waves coursing through me that had nothing to do with the warm water we bathed in. He explored further, finding my clit and all the sweet spots I'd never known existed until him. He took me even higher with each stroke of his fingers until I felt like I was close to bursting with anticipation.

He swept everything off the table set up on one side of the tub. Lifting me up out of the water, he lowered me onto the surface, laying me back. When I tilted my head over the side, I could watch the snow fall through the window.

He spread my legs, hitching my thighs onto his shoulders, and lowered his head. When he sucked on my clit, I released a low keen.

He swirled his tongue around the hard, sensitive bundle of nerves, and I moaned louder. He teased my entrance with light licks before plunging his tongue deep inside me. I arched my back as pleasure rippled through me, tingling down my spine and out to my fingers.

He moved faster, driving his tongue inside me while rolling my clit. I was a bud opening to sunlight for the first time. A rocket blasting across the universe. My hips surged against him, and I held his head in place with my legs as he increased the pressure and angle of his mouth. Every stroke nudged me closer to bliss until I couldn't stand it any longer.

Groaning, I grabbed onto his thick bands of hair, and the soft tips coiled around my wrists, holding tight. Others stroked my belly and thighs.

His low chuckle vibrated through my bones, driving me higher.

When he backed off, I whimpered. But he plunged fingers inside me, and I started spiraling all over again, seeking something I'd never felt before and suspected I'd find only with him.

He paused pumping, gliding his fingers out to run them across my clit, over and over. I couldn't catch my breath. Hunger roared inside me, shooting me into unknown realms of pleasure. When his fingers plunged within me again, his tongue flicked over my clit in circles that seemed to last forever, never quite taking me where I needed to be, still leaving me panting for more.

I writhed beneath him as pleasure pulsed through me so intensely, I thought I might fly apart at any second. He kept going, though—his tongue and lips never straying until my entire body quivered in response to his touch.

When my orgasm came for me, it crashed through me, a blast of wind knocking down everything in its path.

I clung to his hair, moans jerking from my throat as I succumbed, washing away toward the shore.

CHAPTER 20

DARROW

I licked up every drop of her essence, savoring the taste, before easing back to look up at her. "I'm going to do that every day for the rest of my life."

Her laugh jerked out, giddy. "I'm totally spent. I don't believe I'll be able to walk if you do that again."

"I'll carry you everywhere."

"That'll look cute."

"They'll know you're well-loved and feel jealous."

She grinned. Sitting up, she stroked my face. "You're one wonderful surprise after another."

A silly, wild feeling filled me. I wanted to give it free rein. "Time to drag you to—"

Someone knocked on the door.

"Excuse me," a female voice called out. "Princess? Are you in there?"

"Yes," Paige said, her words bubbling with laughter. She slipped into the water but continued to climb out, wrapping the robe around her delectable body, sadly covering it up. She crept over to the door and cracked it open.

I slunk low in the tub. There was no reason I needed to hide, but I cared about her reputation. I wouldn't reveal we were together unless it was her choice.

"Oh, Princess," the woman gushed. I swore I could see her dipping into a low curtsy. "The others asked me to let you know that they're going to light off fireworks out front. They'd love for you to join them. You and the gentleman, Darrow, though I haven't been able to locate him."

"Ah," Paige said. "I believe he took a walk. I'll text him and let him know what's happening."

"Yes, please do, Your Highness. Lady Monica is quite excited."

Paige shut the door and turned, looking my way. "So, do you want to go watch fireworks or create our own here?"

CHAPTER 21

PAIGE

"Both," he said.

Had my longing to stand in the crisp air with him, bundle up, and watch fireworks come through in my tone?

"Let's go join the others," he said. Rising from the tub, he stepped out and wrapped a towel around his waist. He stalked over to me and gently stroked the damp hair off my shoulders. "And then we'll come back here and finish what we started. Fireworks all night long."

"It's a promise." My voice came out breathy. Being with him was all that mattered, but the weekend would be over soon. Maybe I should ditch the fireworks and stay here after all.

"I live to please you," he said.

"You've pleased me more than I could ever imagine." My gaze was drawn to his cock still erect beneath his towel. "It looks like you're missing out, however. Let's just stay here and—"

Another knock rang out on the door.

"Hurry up in there," Rylee called out. "You're going to miss the fireworks!" Her laughter echoed in the hall. "If you don't come out, we'll rouse you."

I was already roused, thank you very much.

"Okay," I said.

The sound of her footsteps headed down the hall.

Darrow kissed me, a deep, heady kiss full of need and passion before he lifted his head. "Hold that thought, because I'm going to bring you back to it."

I nodded, not able to form words.

We dressed quickly and went downstairs. Everyone was already outside, and we joined them, sitting on sofas the staff had brought outside.

"Here you go, Princess," one of the staff said, laying a heated blanket over me and Darrow.

Another staff member came by with hot cider.

"I can't wait," Monica cried, her eyes gleaming as bright as the upcoming fireworks. She nestled in Trevor's arms, staring toward the sky.

Powdery snow drifted through the air, landing on the stone walls and courtyard, creating a pristine winter blanket. The silence of the night was so profound that it magnified the beautiful stillness surrounding us. As if lovingly drawn by unseen hands, the area had been transformed into a magical winter fairytale.

I sucked in the cool, crisp air that was so chilly it made my lungs ache.

Darrow put his arm around my shoulders, and his other hand caressed my thigh, keeping heat simmering inside me. He nuzzled my throat. "You smell amazing, like lust and love and everything wonderful in this world."

Truly, he broke my heart with his words, but with each kiss, he put me back together again.

The stars twinkled dimly overhead, and the shadowy moon cast a soft glow over the landscape. Around us, the trees were adorned with strings of tiny white lights, and the snow sparkled in the light of lanterns swaying in the light breeze.

A loud bang filled the air. I gasped as a fountain of sparks lit up the sky in front of us, followed by a beautiful array of colors. Rockets of red, blue, green, and yellow filled the night. They seemed to reach all the way to the stars.

"Amazing," Darrow said, equally stunned. His hand took mine, holding tight.

"Ah," Monica cried during a pause. "It's so pretty. Thank you, Trevor, my gorgeous, amazing husband. Thank you, Elisa and Raze for making this weekend so special. And thank you, my friends, for sharing this wonderful time with us."

"It's so lovely," Rylee said, snuggling into Gunner's side. His arm wrapped around her, and he held the blanket up to her chin, keeping her warm.

"So glad I could be here," Elisa said, Raze's deep voice echoing her words. They sat side by side but apart. Had they made any headway in finding common ground to stand on?

Multiple whooshes filled the night again, and we gasped as the rockets shot into the sky, exploding for our pleasure. The show mesmerized me, and my eyes widened as each new blast of color lit up the sky. If only I could catch each one in my hand, a colorful firefly that I could keep forever.

The show came to an end, but we remained in place, grinning at each other, sharing this perfect moment. The snow began to fall again in gentle, sparkling flakes that glistened on the ground and trees.

"It's over," Monica said with a sigh. "So pretty. I don't believe my honeymoon weekend could be more complete."

"Oh, no?" Trevor asked with a happy growl. He stood and swept her up into his arms, holding her tight with the blanket wrapped around her. He strode toward the entrance, and the staff swept open the front door. "I think I should show you how this weekend can get better."

"So romantic," Rylee said in a wistful voice.

Gunner, taking a cue from his cousin, swept her up and did the same, striding inside the castle.

Before I could joke to Darrow about testing out the strength of his arms, he lifted me and spun around. Stopping, he kissed me, his lips cool from the snow, his mouth warm from our growing heat.

He strode through the front door, and I peeked over my shoulder at Elisa and Raze.

He stared at his hands clasped on his lap, then subtly

peeked at her. He wasn't wearing his glasses. Contacts? Damn, he had incredibly long lashes and pretty green eyes.

Her face full of longing, Elisa didn't seem to notice his attention.

They seemed like nice people, and maybe it was overly romantic of me, but I wanted everyone to feel the way I did nestled in Darrow's arms.

As if life couldn't get any better.

DARROW

Paige's fingers teased the nape of my neck as we climbed the stairs.

I carried her easily, but my heart was on fire. Finally, after all these years and lost dreams, we would be together. What we'd done so far would pale in comparison to what we were about to do.

We stopped outside her door, and she gave me a shy smile. When we'd left to watch the fireworks, our bodies had still been aflame.

"Take me inside, Darrow," she said softly, the heady gleam in her eyes telling me she wanted me.

What had I done to deserve such perfection?

I nodded and entered her room.

Someone had come while we were gone and drained the tub, though they'd left the candles burning and replenished the tray. The ice cream had long since melted, but in its place, they'd left chocolate covered strawberries.

I lowered Paige to her feet. She strolled to the tray while I shut and locked the door, then returned with a berry she fed me.

"I note chocolate," she said in a heady voice.

"It tastes wonderful, but not as good as you, love." Did she mind that I called her that? From the widening of her smile, I'd say no.

Paige put her arms around me, nuzzling my chest.

"I want you." Emotion filled my voice, making it come out hoarser than I liked. My thick bands of hair, so startling at first but now welcome because they were a part of me, coiled out, stroking her cheek.

She stepped back and, with an eager grin, tugged off her sweater. Her shirt. She shimmied out of her pants and underwear. Straightening, she watched me.

Heat coiled along my bones, scorching me wherever it touched.

I ripped away my clothing, not caring if they tore.

The room was silent as my eyes searched her body. I loved the lush curve of her hips, her ass, and her generous breasts. She was my beautiful angel, and I wanted to devour her. I wanted to make her feel good in every way that I could. I wanted to show her pleasure like she'd never experienced before. My heart thrummed with anticipation and a desire to make her happy.

Without a word, I reached out and touched her cheek. I cupped it in my palm and caressed her skin with my thumb, feeling her warmth. My cock stiffened as I continued to look into her eyes, falling deeper and deeper into her gaze.

My other hand slowly moved to her neck. I tugged her closer, gliding the back of my fingers down her body, feeling her curves and dips, wanting nothing more than to feel her entire body. She watched my face, her fingers stroking my chest, moving down to my cock.

She trembled as my fingers lightly caressed her.

Leaning in, I pressed my lips against hers, feeling them part and invite me in. She ran her hands along my cock with broad strokes, setting me aflame.

I kissed her jaw and down her chest, pausing to suck on each of her nipples. She pressed her chest forward, her head falling back and her moan echoing around us.

I flicked her nipples with my tongue, and her moans grew louder.

My fingers moved down her body, and I gently eased them between her legs.

She spread her thighs, quivering as I stroked her clit and pushed my fingers inside her.

My cock was a steel rod banging against my abs. I couldn't wait much longer.

With a heady groan, she arched toward me. I kissed my way across her rounded belly and spread her legs. When I licked her and focused my attention on her clit, she whimpered. Her fingers clutched my hair that coiled around her wrists.

I stabbed my tongue inside her along with my fingers, and she thrust toward me, holding my hair tight.

When her gasps grew more urgent, I stood and lifted her up, pressing her against the wall. Her legs wrapped around me as I centered my cock at her core.

One thrust, and I impaled myself inside her welcoming heat.

CHAPTER 23

PAIGE

He lifted me and pressed me against the wall. It was all I could do to think. I'd crested the edge of a cliff, and it wouldn't take much to drive me down the other side.

Gazing into my eyes, he nudged my entrance with the thick head of his cock.

I wrapped my legs around him, tugging him near.

"Paige," he whispered. "Love."

With one thrust, he buried his long length inside me.

My body quaked as waves of pleasure surged through me, and with it came an emotion even more powerful than the physical sensations—a deep, unyielding connection between us.

His gaze never wavered from mine. His passion was a force of nature, radiating from his body and engulfing me in its intensity. He pulled out slowly, then thrust forward again, moving with slow, sure strokes that were deliberate and full of caring.

The heat of the moment built until it was almost too much to bear.

My head spun with pleasure like I'd stepped onto a dizzying carnival ride. Overriding it all were his eyes never leaving mine, a gaze so passionate it seemed to penetrate every part of me.

My skin flushed with desire as he pushed deeper and faster into me, driving the intensity higher until I thought I would burst from it.

We lost control. Our bodies moved as one, our hips meeting with each thrust, pushing us higher and higher. The wonder of being with my first and last love consumed me.

With each movement, he whispered my name. His hands explored my body with reverence, but his gaze never left mine, communicating without words the strength of his emotions for me.

My skin flushed, and heat radiated outward from where we were joined.

We reached the peak together, and with one final push, we shattered. We were left clinging to each other, breathless and trembling with the aftermath of our love.

And in that moment, I realized how deeply he cared for me, not only in how he made love to me, but because of the way he looked at me with such tenderness. His eyes shone with adoration, as if nothing else mattered more to him than this moment between us.

I woke the next morning resting in his arms with sunlight slanting through the room. His arms tightened around me, telling me he guessed I was awake.

Rising over him, I gazed into his gorgeous teal eyes that I sensed could wield destruction at a whim. Now, they only held love and hope.

I stroked him, savoring the nubs on the sides of his cock. They quivered. Soon, I was caught up in the wonder of just being with him. Straddling him, I sunk down onto his length, taking all of him inside me.

We moved together slowly at first and with exquisite tenderness before our emotions caught up with us. He lifted hard to meet me, holding my hips to drive me down on his length.

Finding my clit, he rolled it, his eyes remaining locked on mine.

Too soon, I got caught up in the moment. It rushed over me, engulfing me. I collapsed on his chest as he pumped inside me a few more times before his groan rang out in the room.

"I don't know where this is going," he said softly against my hair. "We haven't talked about a future. But I want you to know that I'm with you no matter where you choose to go. I only want to be by your side, Paige."

"Darrow," I said, my voice heavy with emotion. With him so much taller than me, I couldn't reach his mouth, so I peppered kisses on his chest. "Do you want me to move here to be with you or do you want to join me in Monsterville?"

He rolled until I was beneath him and cupped my face. "Do you mean it? Us, together, forever?"

I grinned. "I can't imagine anything better than being with you."

He kissed me, and heat spiraled between us. His fingers—

Someone knocked on the door.

"This is turning into a bad habit," he said with a soft laugh.

"Excuse me, Princess?" a female voice called out. "Lady Monica asked me to come wake you. She said I was to rouse you—"

"There's that word again," I said.

"Aren't you already . . . roused?" Darrow whispered in my ear.

I nodded. I sure was. Very roused.

"Breakfast is waiting, and then everyone's going sledding on the front lawn," the woman said. "Can I tell her you'll be down?"

"Yes," I called out. "I'd love to go sledding."

"Lord Darrow didn't answer my knock. Should I try again to rouse him as well, perhaps with a louder knock?"

"I'll, um, rouse him," I said, winking at him. "Thank you anyway!"

"Very well," she said. "I'll tell Lady Monica you'll be down promptly." Her footsteps faded in the hall.

"Prompt is a relative term, right?" I asked him.

"With you, I can be very prompt." He lifted a bottle of chocolate sauce off the bedside table and grinned as he trickled some out onto my breast. Then he proceeded to lick it off.

After showering and dressing, we joined everyone at breakfast, filling plates at the buffet.

Grannie Vi and Uncle Bub had opted to sleep in, but the rest of our friends chattered about going sledding. After we finished, we put on our winter clothing and went outside where Bart greeted us on the front lawn, holding hands with Poppy.

Bright blue and yellow plastic sleds clustered around him.

"If you'll come over here, I'll explain," he said, shifting his hooves in the snow as we strolled across the drive. "Select a sled. Couples or single; it doesn't matter. There are enough sleds to go around."

He waved a hoof to the steep hill behind him. Beyond a long stretch of snow, a forest waited, but the land sloped upward before then, which would make it easier to come to a stop without plowing through the brush. "When you reach the bottom," he said, "staff will be waiting to bring you and your sleds back to the top. Any questions?"

We all shrugged, stomping our feet in excitement.

"Ride together?" Darrow asked, squeezing my mitten-clad hand.

At my nod, he selected a long yellow sled, and we climbed on board, him sitting behind me, his arm wrapped around my waist and his heels sticking out at the sides.

The thick snow glinted in the sunlight as we perched atop the hill.

Bart and Poppy took off first. She lifted her hands overhead, squealing while he controlled the sled.

My heart thudded against my chest wall, the anticipation of what was to come making my pulse flutter. I took a deep breath, inhaling the stunning winter air, the tang of pine, and the crisp cold scent of snow. Snow didn't actually smell like anything, but that was how it seemed.

Inching us forward, Darrow's arm tightened around me. "Hold on!" He gave us a gentle push, and we were off, gliding down the hill slowly at first before picking up speed.

Around us, our friends soared down the slope as well. Rylee rode with Gunner, and Monica with Trevor, but Elisa and Raze had chosen separate sleds.

The snow crunched beneath us. A thrill coursed through my veins as we went faster, my hair flying out behind me, the cold winter air hitting my face with a thousand prickles.

Darrow hooted, and my voice joined in. I lifted my arms in the air and gave in to the amazing sensation of flying across the snow.

My laughter rang out, muffled by the wind. I'd never felt so alive, so exhilarated, so incredibly happy. Being with Darrow was all that mattered.

We hit a rise and lifted off the ground, bumping back

down before my gasp could pop out. Laughing, we continued sliding, heading for the incline where we leveled off and slowed.

The low rumble of an engine rang out, breaking through the moment. A black sedan drove sedately up the driveway, passing us.

Our sled came to a stop as the car halted in front of the castle.

Darrow climbed off the sled and held his gloved hand out to help me to my feet. Staff rushed over to take the sled from him.

"This way," a female gargoyle said, her wings fluttering out before settling against her spine. She held open the back door to a three-rowed SUV, and Darrow and I climbed inside, joining the others.

The gargoyle took the driver's seat and returned us to the front of the castle.

While our friends hurried to the hill to slide again, the front doors of the black car opened. A couple climbed out.

My breath caught.

I gaped at my parents.

CHAPTER 24

DARROW

I waited with Paige as her parents strode over to join us, not sure how I felt. Part of me wanted to rage at them while another part of me only felt sadness. I knew why they'd taken her away, but that did nothing to stop my anger from blooming inside me.

"Paige," Francine said, her voice fluttering, her hands outstretched to her daughter as if she'd snatch her away once more. This time, they'd make sure we never saw each other again.

I hadn't seen Francine and Franklin in ten years, but they didn't look much different from when I'd been invited to dinner often and when I'd felt welcome enough to stroll inside their house after school and raid the cookie jar sitting on the kitchen counter.

Their faces tightened as they stopped in front of us.

"You need to leave with us right now," Francine said, turning her pleading gaze to Paige. "Please. He'll hurt you."

Paige leaned into my side. "Darrow would never do anything like that. You're the ones who hurt me. How could you take me from Petrified Woods when you knew how much he meant to me?"

"He'll turn you to stone," Franklin hissed, his hand spiking in my direction. "Look at him. He's a medusa. A monster."

"The only monsters here are you two," Paige said. Her voice broke. "I can't believe you did that to me. To Darrow. I loved him, and you stole me from him."

My heart surged to hear her standing up for me, to hear of her love. She was sticking up for us.

"He's a hideous beast," Francine snarled. "Look at his hair." Her finger snapped out to flick one of the strands, and the rest responded to my anger, flaring out around my head. She gasped. "It's alive! He has snakes on his head, and his skin's the color of ashes. Never look into his eyes. They'll turn on you and it will be over!"

"Come with us. Please," Franklin said, his voice leveling. "Leave him here with the other monsters."

Paige lifted her chin. "I won't. I'm an adult. I make my own decisions, and I'm staying with Darrow."

Francine turned her sharp eyes my way, impaling me on the spot. "How many?" she barked.

"Excuse me?" Paige asked, her confused gaze shooting from me to her parents.

Lead solidified in my gut. Like an airplane spiraling toward the ground, there was no stopping me from crashing.

"How many?" Franklin cried. "Or is it too many to count by now?"

"Seventeen," I said, my voice dull. I knew very well what they meant.

"And now you're going to make it eighteen," Francine said, her voice lifting to a shriek. "Twenty if we continue to stand in your way, am I correct?"

"What are they talking about?" Paige asked, a whimper coming through in her voice.

I stared at the ground. If I didn't, I'd release the wrath boiling inside me on them. The ground beneath my feet shifted, flexing as it turned to stone.

"Look," Francine cried, reeling backward, away from the rock forming beneath her feet. "Look! He's doing it before our very eyes." She rushed forward and yanked on Paige's arm, but my love remained standing beside me.

Would she stay with me if she knew what I'd done?

"I've learned to control it," I said stiffly.

"It doesn't appear that way to me," Franklin said.

"*I* make it happen," I said, pleading for them to understand. "It's not the other way around."

Franklin stomped closer, his face so ruddy, I thought he'd explode. "Seventeen doesn't show any control at all. Look at the ground. Your hands are clenched. You're a hideous monster about to rampage through everything in sight."

"Please," Paige said to me. "What are they talking about?"

"He's turned seventeen people to stone with one look

in his eyes," Francine said with a sneer. "He's a horrible beast. You'll be next, Paige. Mark my words."

"You turned seventeen people to stone?" Paige asked, her shoulders curling forward. "*Seventeen?*"

I couldn't bear the accusation in her eyes.

While she gaped at me, I pivoted on my heel and stalked along the path winding around the castle.

When I hit the end of the building, I turned toward the back of the castle and bolted.

"Darrow," I called after him, my heart crushed and my world falling apart. "Darrow!"

He didn't turn back. No, he walked faster, breaking into a run when he reached the side of the castle, and disappearing around the corner.

"See?" Mom said, her grip tightening on my arm. "He's running, which is much better than turning all of us to stone. We'll quickly pack your things and get you out of here. I'm sorry you had to discover what a wretch he is, but perhaps it's for the best."

Dad shot me a solemn look. "He took advantage of your sweet ways, honey, but it's over. We'll take you where he'll never find you again."

"That's why you moved away so fast, isn't it?" I asked.

"Within a week after being rescued from the scientist's lab, he'd solidified two poor souls, and we knew you'd be next," Mom said. "How else could we protect you?"

My eyes stung with tears, and I tried to break free, but her fingers bit into my skin. Just like ten years ago, they'd make a choice for me without giving me a say. "You took me from him when he needed me more than anyone else."

"Let's not be dramatic," Mom said. "You were sixteen, a child. You had no clue about life or about those who could cause you true harm."

"He was changed, and that was it," Dad said. "The Darrow you knew then died, and he was replaced with a silver monster who can kill with one glance. We had no choice. It was leave or let him turn that horrible gaze on you."

"I wasn't a child," I said, peering toward the side of the castle, hoping he'd come back. "I loved him. I *still* love him. And I'm going to go find him and tell him."

I yanked away from Mom and took off down the path, flinging my arms out to keep from falling on the slippery walkway.

"Darrow," I cried, whirling around the side of the building just in time to see him stepping inside the maze far up the hill.

He didn't look my way.

I raced after him, wishing my boots had cleats, my feet skidding this way and that. Short of breath and my cheeks freezing, I finally reached the maze. I raced down the path on the right and turned at the corner, slowly making my way toward the center—or where I believed the center must be.

"Darrow," I called, but he still didn't reply. This reminded me of when he'd chased me, and I'd hid inside the maze. I was hurt, and I imagined he was now. "Darrow? Darrow! I'm not giving up. I told my parents off and as far as I know, they're leaving. Without me. You hear that? Without me! I'm staying here even if that means I'll freeze to death in the maze, though I hope you'll find me and warm me back up. Jeez, where are you? Why won't you speak with me?"

I came to a halt at a dead end and backtracked to an intersection, peering in both directions. Unsure which way to go, I looked up, trying to gauge where I was inside the maze. If I guessed correctly, the center was to my left —one or two rows of hedge away.

Well, if you couldn't beat 'em . . .

I climbed up onto a bench and launched myself up and over the row of hedges.

With a guttural cry, I flipped over.

The ground rushed toward me, and . . .

CHAPTER 26

DARROW

I was right to leave her with her parents. If I'd stayed with her, I would've begged. There was nothing wrong with begging, but I wanted her to make the decision to leave with them or stay here with me on her own.

Doing what they did would be wrong. I'd never force her to be with me.

So why, then, was I sitting on a bench in the middle of the maze, freezing my ass off while she called my name, trying to find her way to the center?

Eh, I was chickenshit, still stuck in the past, a teenage kid who thought he had everything, only to have it stolen away.

"Darrow? Darrow!" she cried.

I remained on the bench.

Yup, definitely chickenshit.

"I'm not giving up," she said. "I told my parents off and as far as I know, they're leaving. Without me. You hear that? Without me! I'm staying here even if that means I'll freeze to death in the maze without you, though I hope you'll warm me back up. Jeez, where are you? Why won't you speak with me?"

Her voice faded to nothing, and when I didn't hear her moving or her calling out again, I began to believe she'd left.

That was when she launched herself up over a hedge.

Gulping, I leapt from the bench and flung myself toward her, catching her before she hit the ground.

I strode back to the bench, sitting with her in my arms. If I was wise, I'd put her down. Let her decide if she wanted to be held by me or not.

She looked up at me. "Hey."

"Hey." I blinked, unsure what to say.

"I know your life has been rough for the past ten years," she said. "I wish I could go back in time and run away from my parents and find you. I'd hold you and tell you everything was going to be okay. I'm sorry. I should've questioned everything when they told me you were dead."

It was time I told her everything. Only then could she truly decide what she wanted to do. If she chose to walk away, I'd let her go. At least she'd do so with all the information.

"After I was kidnapped, the scientist put me inside a machine. I felt the waves across my skin. Then I was rescued. I thought it was over, but the day after that, I woke up with silver skin and this hair." I flicked one of the thick strands, and it snaked toward her before settling back on my shoulder. "I thought, okay, cool, I can live with this. But then a neighbor came to visit Dad. One look from me, and he turned to stone."

"Darrow," she said softly, her arms going around my shoulders.

"Mom took off, not saying goodbye. Dad stayed, but I don't think he ever looked at me in the same way again." I spoke stoically, having come to a feeling of peace about what happened after that. Back then, though, I'd been as horrified as everyone else. "As soon as I realized what I'd done, I ran. But I'm human even if only on the inside, and I need to be around people as much as anyone else. I crept back to my home, telling myself I could control it, that I'd make sure my eyes didn't do it again. But they did. Soon there was another statue standing on my lawn, both of their faces locked in fear. I did that to them."

"You don't do it any longer."

"Oh, I do," I said, my rueful laugh slipping out. "Only now, when it happens, it's because I want it to. Anyone I change nowadays is done on purpose."

"How did two people turn into seventeen?" she asked.

"You heard that, huh?"

"Was it an accident?" Only sympathy and understanding came through in her voice, and it hurt so much to hear it. I ached to be with her. Loved by her. I wanted to show her that her faith in me mattered.

"I changed the last group to help someone else." I explained about my friend, a wolf shifter, and his mate, and how her mafia family tracked her down and attacked them. That I'd gone to the battle to support them with our other friends, and I changed all the mafia lord's henchmen into stone and hauled them to Petrified Woods.

"Now you have a bunch of statues on your front lawn?" Even now, she didn't sound horrified. I swore laughter tinkled in her voice.

Did we stand a chance of a future together?

"I can control it now," I said. "I figured that out before I turned seventeen. And even better, I know how to reverse it. Those neighbors? They're no longer statues, and while they don't easily meet my eye, we're still friends. They know I didn't mean to do it and they forgave me."

"What about the mafia henchmen?"

"Oh, I've returned most of them to their human form. They agreed to find new careers and leave my friends alone."

"Most."

"One of them still isn't ready to cooperate."

"I see. Seems like he needs more time inside stone, then." She grinned up at me and tightened her arms around my shoulders. That's when I realized she wasn't frightened of what I could do. She wasn't running away. The joy of it hit me like a stone block in the forehead, waking me up.

"You're not leaving," I said in wonder.

"Do you want me to?"

I shook my head. And I kissed her.

She moaned when our mouths met, turning to press herself against me, to link her legs around me. Her warmth infused me with flames, and I took in her heady scent and the taste of her passion.

My eyes closed as I savored the feeling of her caressing my shoulders, arms, and back.

When we finally pulled apart, a wave of love washed over me. My heart pounded. Looking into her eyes, I saw the love I felt reflected at me.

"I love you, Darrow," she said. "I'm not going anywhere unless you push me away."

"You don't need to worry about that, because I'm never pushing. I love you too, Paige. Always have, and nothing is ever going to change that."

A feeling of completeness filled me.

"Why don't we go up to your room or mine, fill the tub, and climb into it?" she said. "Oh, and chocolate sauce. I think there might be some left in the bottle."

"There's no other way I want to spend my afternoon," I said, standing with her still in my arms.

"Then take me back to the castle, Darrow, so I can have my way with you, and you can do the same with me," she said with a grin.

And we did.

CHAPTER 27

EPILOGUE
THE FOLLOWING SPRING

Paige

"Put it in there," I told our orc friend, Max, as he passed me carrying a box from the moving van out front. I leaped up and stroked the silky black hair of his half-human daughter, Sydnee, riding in a baby carrier on his back. She gurgled and grinned.

Darrow paused as he followed Max down the hall and gave me a kiss. When he backed away, his adoring gaze took in the ring sparkling on my left hand.

"Can't wait for our wedding, love," he whispered, lifting me off my feet in a big hug.

Until we could set everything up for our wedding (using Elisa and Raze's wedding planner services), we were moving in together. We'd bought a cute house in Monsterville a few doors down from Chastity and Max.

"That deck," Chastity said, coming in from outside, "I froze my butt off out there, but it was worth it to take in the view." Her head tilted as she looked Max's way. "I think their view is even nicer than ours, honey. What do you think?"

Sydnee chortled and kicked her feet when she saw her mom.

"Nothing beats our view." Max grinned, shaking his head as he continued down the hall with her right behind.

The front door burst open, and Poppy and Bart rushed inside, their arms full of potted plants.

"We got them inside as fast as we could," Poppy said, peering around for a place to set down a plant. "Where should we put them?"

I waved to the living room on my left. "Maybe near the wall? I'll move them around later once I've figured out where I'm putting the couch."

After they put the plants down, Bart swept Poppy up in his arms. While she squealed, he carried her through the front door. If I knew them, it might be a little while before they returned with more of my plants they'd transported in their car. They'd eloped two weeks ago, and she was now helping him run his castle wedding venue. She wore long dresses every day, settling into her role as the castle's new queen.

He'd convinced (I think) his staff that I wasn't a princess, though one of the women recently messaged me expressing sadness that my right to rule had been wrenched away from me. She said she'd be happy to start a social media campaign on my behalf, demanding my reinstatement as the heir to the throne. I'd thanked her and told her I was happy to live incognito, but that I truly wasn't a princess. She hadn't replied.

"We need help out here," Grannie Vi called from the front lawn. "You need to tell us where Raze should put . . . Is that a real person or just a statue? I swear, between Darrow's statuary business, his carvings, and those vague rumors about medusas, it's darn near hard to tell."

Darrow and I snorted at each other before donning coats and mittens and hurrying outside.

Grannie Vi and Uncle Bub stood on the walk, bundled up in thick, matching coats with white fuzz around the hoods. They leaned on their canes, watching as Raze single-handedly carried a statue of a man across his shoulder, his shiny black shoes thudding down the ramp of the big moving truck. Even now, he wore a designer suit, though it looked great on him, giving him an air of sophistication despite his burly ogre appearance.

"I think Raze should put it with the leprechauns," Grannie Vi said, pointing her cane to the cluster of knee-high figures standing beneath a leafless tree. One of them moved. I think. I frowned but couldn't tell. Leprechauns hadn't joined the human world, had they?

Raze started in that direction with the statue, his glasses already fogging up from the chilly air.

"Actually," Bub said, pointing in the opposite direction. "Maybe he should put it with the deer." He squinted. "Are those real deer? Darn, but they're lifelike. Amazing work, there, Darrow."

Raze turned and stomped through the snow in the opposite direction.

"They're not real," Darrow called out, taking my hand and squeezing it. He bought plastic lawn figures from a phoenix who'd moved to town, then turned them to stone. We thought it might be fun to set up a full Christmas display on the lawn and include nine reindeer. We'd smile whenever we looked at it, and it would be great advertising for the statuary business Darrow was opening here in Monsterville.

"They darn well look real," Bub said, shaking his head. "We need to get inside before we freeze our patooties off, right, Elvira?"

At her nod, they hobbled up the walk and passed us, entering the house.

"You can put him down . . ." Darrow frowned Raze's way. "Well, wherever you'd like."

With a grunt, Raze lowered the statue beside the walk. The stone guy stared toward the road, his hand lifted and his finger pointing. The scowl he'd worn the last time Darrow unfroze him remained. He still wasn't willing to leave our friends, Luna and Storm, alone, so he would remain stone until we loosened him up again this spring.

Raze frowned as he stared at the statue, his head tilting. He pushed his glasses up as he leaned close to study the guy's face, gnawing on his upper lip with his tusks. "This must be some of Darrow's art. I'm not confident I fully understand what you're aiming for with it, however."

"That one's called Contemplation," Darrow said. "I believe someday, I'll be able to change his name to Redemption."

Raze grunted. His gaze sought Elisa who'd come out onto the deck, holding Sydnee in her arms. She sang softly to the little girl while Sydnee kicked her feet and squealed. The longing in Raze's stoic gaze made my heart ache. Over the past month, they hadn't come to any kind of agreement as far as I could tell, but I still had hope something wonderful would develop between them.

"I spoke with Venom," Darrow told me quietly.

"On the phone?" I asked.

"Can you picture Venom speaking on a phone?"

Grinning, I shook my head. "Well, no. But even demons need to communicate with people who aren't standing in front of them."

"I imagine he can pop himself just about anywhere if he needs to have a conversation," Darrow said. "I saw him in town this morning, though. When I explained our situation, he told me he'd stop by later and see if he could persuade our stone man to cooperate. Things might get heated out here."

A demon. Heated. My laughter rang out, and everyone looked my way. "What?" I asked, splaying my hands wide. "I'm happy."

Darrow's arm went around my shoulder, and he kissed the top of my head. "Me too. Couldn't be any happier."

"Casserole," Rylee called out, rushing up the walk with Gunner and their little boy, Josh, right behind her. "I made you dinner." She stopped beside us, grinning. "Where should I put it?"

"On the counter in the kitchen. Thank you so much," I said. Storm and Luna had stopped by earlier with food from Storm's restaurant, plus Violet and Goreg came by with scones and muffins. At this rate, we'd have enough food for a month.

After carrying the rest of our things inside, we thanked everyone profusely for their help and said goodbye.

We locked the front door and leaned against it, smiling as we took in the mess we'd have to sort through before our lives would be settled.

Darrow turned and cupped my cheeks. His gorgeous teal eyes met mine. "What should we eat for dinner, love?"

"Hmm." I grinned. "I believe we still have some chocolate sauce in the fridge."

I hope you've enjoyed Darrow & Paige's story!
Check out the rest of the Monsterville, USA world…

Orc Me Baby One More Time
(Gunner & Rylee)
If you've already read
Orc Me Baby One More Time,

get your FREE Bonus Chapters!
Rylee & Gunner are having a baby!

Candy For My Orc Boss
(Max & Chastity)

Gargoyles Just Want to Have Fun
(Violet & Goreg)

AND, if you'd like a peek at
Uptown Ogre,
Raze & Elisa's story,
keep scrolling . . .

ABOUT THE AUTHOR

Ava Ross is a two-time *USA Today* Bestselling author who has written numerous titles, all of them featuring sweet and steamy romance. She fell for men with unusual features when she first watched Star Wars, where alien creatures have gone mainstream. She lives in New England with her husband (who is sadly not an alien, though he is still cute in his own way), her kids, and a few assorted pets.

SERIES BY AVA

Mail-Order Brides of Crakair

Brides of Driegon

Fated Mates of the Ferlaern Warriors

Fated Mates of the Xilan Warriors

Holiday with a Cu'zod Warrior

Galaxy Games

Alien Warrior Abandoned

Beastly Alien Boss

Bride of the Fae

A Sci-fi Holiday Tail

Monsterville, USA

Monster on Board
(Co-written with Alana Khan)

A Monster Worth Fighting For
(Monster Between the Sheets)

Love at First Orc

Third Galaxy on the Left

You can find my books on Amazon.

UPTOWN OGRE

A suit-wearing ogre is pretending to be my boyfriend, and I think I'm falling in love.

After being ousted from my small town by an underhanded wedding planner who is also now my ex, I moved to Monsterville for a fresh start. There, I find myself in direct competition with the hottest ogre in town, Raze. He's too cocky and snobby for his own good, and he wears designer suits and ties all the time. I sometimes wonder if he wears them to bed.

When my ex shows up in Monsterville, determined to win me back, Raze steps in, offering to pretend he's my boyfriend and business partner. Only when my ex tries to outbid me on a royal fae wedding do I agree. With our combined forces, Raze and I will win the job and send my ex packing.

The more time I spend with Raze, however, the more I wish he was my real boyfriend. Can I convince him that an ogre and a human are the perfect monster match?

Uptown Ogre is set in the Monsterville, USA Series. Each book is standalone and is best if read in order (see below). Expect romantic hijinks with monsters, heat, and a happily ever after.

Check out the entire Monsterville world!

Candy for my Orc Boss
Orc Me Baby One More Time
Gargoyles Just Want to Have Fun
Don't Go Knotting My Heart
Whose Bed Have Your Claws Been Under?
Uptown Ogre
Oops, I Elf'd it Again
My Orc-y Breaky Heart
Hold Me Closer, Fiery Phoenix
Who Let the Demon Out?

CHAPTER 1

ELISA

Raze, my ogre wedding planner competition who happened to own an office across from mine, opened the door to *my* office and stepped inside. He brought with him a welcome gust of spring mountain air and his unwelcome surly attitude.

I hadn't seen him since Christmas, when we formed a truce only long enough to plan the wedding for his cousin and my friend. After that, we returned to Monsterville and tried to ignore each other.

He hated me. If only I could hate him. Leave it to me to form a crush on the guy who ran the only other wedding planner business in town. The last time something like that happened . . . Well, that was why I'd moved to Monsterville for a fresh start.

Despite his perpetual scowl, I struggled not to notice how well this ogre body filled out his suit. At five-nine, I was tall, but he towered over me by at least a foot. A girl should be turned off by his copper skin and knobby ogre head, let alone his horns, but I couldn't look away. He kept his hair cut short, which fit with his business-ogre image.

Most of the monsters living in town were equally broad and muscular. I should hook up with one of them, right?

Now that monsters had melted out of the woods and clawed their way up from beneath the ground, joining human society, I could have my pick from hot, winged gargoyles, feisty centaurs with more than one . . . ahem, and even a few grumpy trolls eager to make me pay an interesting price to cross their bridge.

Why couldn't I fixate on one of them instead of Raze?

"Can I help you?" I asked him, my voice higher-pitched than I liked.

"Finish what you're doing." He waved a manicured hand to my clients sitting across the desk from me, and his tail swept back and forth behind him. "I'll wait. We can speak after you're finished."

The woman gawked at him, and I could see why. Even if he was a snob, he kind of blew you away.

"Check out the ogre," the bride, Margie, whispered to her orc fiancé. "You should wear a suit like that to the wedding."

Her family was well-connected in town, and scoring this job would give my fledgling business the boost it needed. Instead of sitting at my desk forlornly staring at my silent phone, I would be booking one wedding after another. If I was awarded this job and the fae wedding I was about to bid on, my reputation would be set.

Vrok patted the cute dragonette sitting on his shoulder, and it preened before shooting Margie a scowl—or what I took for a scowl. She ignored it, which was odd since his family raised them, and he and Margie were engaged. You'd think she'd be interested in the creature since they were so closely linked to his family.

When I first saw his dragonette, I was mesmerized by the tiny creature's golden scales and the spit of flames it shot my way in affection.

Vrok turned to peer over his shoulder at Raze, keeping his voice low when he spoke with his fiancé. "Do you think I'd look good in a black suit with a starched shirt and tie?" He didn't sound convinced, though he should get used to the idea because other than the color, Margie had made it clear he'd be wearing a suit at their wedding.

"Trust me." She tapped her long nails on his arm. "I understand things like this when you . . . sometimes don't."

Oh-oh. Was there trouble between them? I'd hate to lose this job, but their happiness came first.

He nodded. "I'll try." And that was all anyone could ask for in a relationship.

As for the stiff ogre still standing in my doorway, I'd yet to see Raze dressed in anything but designer suits. Did he ever let down his hair, so to speak, and wear something casual?

Doubtful. I could picture him sitting upright on his porch or deck or whatever he might have at his home, still dressed like a billionaire businessman. No beer in his hand. No games set up on the lawn. And definitely no cute little doggies or dragonettes curling up on his lap.

For all I knew, he slept in a suit. I could barely resist the urge to stride over to him and loosen his tie, maybe undo a couple of the top buttons of his shirt and expose his chest.

Oh, and tug off his glasses so I could stare into his gorgeous green eyes.

Sadly, my inconsistent crush was not returned. Inconsistent, that is, because I went from wanting to kiss him to an insatiable urge to kill him.

I had nothing against ogres in general, just one very irritating ogre wedding planner who was determined to drive me out of business. Five months ago, when I moved to Monsterville and set up shop, he'd done his best to make me leave town, reminding me too much of why I'd closed my prior business and slunk here.

"So," I said to my clients. "You said you want to serve pink pasta with a pink-colored alfredo sauce." I struggled not to cringe. The customer was always right, and Raze was listening. I had to show him I could provide a valuable service.

Handling this well would show the fae family I was the perfect planner for their upcoming royal wedding. They'd accept my bid, and my position as the reigning wedding planner in town would be secured.

Raze leaned against the wall beside the door and watched me, his arms crossing on his chest.

"As you can tell, my fiancée really loves pink," Vrok said. I got the impression he was trying not to cringe. "If it makes Margie happy, I'm all about pink."

Margie leaned forward. "I was thinking of pink balloons and using some of that shimmery draping cloth as an archway when we enter the reception."

Raze released an odd sound, and I shot him a glare. Really, couldn't he come back when I wasn't busy? Or a year from now when I was completely established and could look down my nose at him instead of the other way around?

We'd been adversaries from the moment we met, when we were forced to co-organize the Christmas wedding. My friend, Monica, hired me to plan her side of the wedding to her ogre fiancé, Trevor. Trevor hired his snooty ogre cousin, Raze, to help me coordinate the weekend events. We'd spent half the time arguing and the rest of the time dreaming up what we could argue about next.

I couldn't imagine why my friend, Paige, suggested he liked me.

Raze cleared his throat as if he suspected I was daydreaming about his muscles. I had been earlier, but I wasn't now.

Margie grinned and patted Vrok's arm again. "Yes, I want lots of pink." She leaned against his side, linking their fingers. "Pink tablecloths, and pink flowers."

"Ah," I said. "Perhaps with white baby's breath to break up the pink?"

Margie frowned. "Oh, no, we want everything to be pink."

I nodded, though I was trying to figure out how we could keep their reception from looking like a Pepto Bismol explosion. "The walls and floor of your venue won't be pink, of course."

Margie frowned and her voice lifted to a screech. "Why can't they be pink too?"

"Because we're only renting the room for the day," Vrok said, and I admired his patience. "Their next clients might prefer another color."

She blinked slowly at him as if she was seeing him for the first time.

"You could drape cloth on the floor and walls," she said, shooting a glance toward Raze who continued to watch us. Didn't he have his own clients to chat with? "Other wedding planners have said they could do this," she added.

Damn him, was he poaching on my client? The ink was barely dry on my contract with Margie and Vrok. They were still within the one-week back-out window. To succeed in my new business, I needed every job I could get. I was barely making the rent on my office as it is.

I shot Raze a warning glare, receiving only a lifted unibrow look in exchange.

"Let me speak with your wedding venue," I said quickly. "I'm sure something can be arranged."

"Maybe . . ." Vrok shook his head.

"What?" Margie snapped his way.

"Nothing." He slumped in his chair.

I tugged my list over to make sure we went through the rest of the items on my agenda. "Pink champagne, naturally."

Margie's smile returned, and my pulse lowered to a more normal level.

"In addition to pink pasta and alfredo sauce, I'll ensure they serve rosy bread with stained butter. I spoke with Storm, the wolf shifter catering the event, and he's excited about the radish-beet salad he'll prepare to go with the main course."

"Yay." Margie wiggled in her seat, clapping her hands.

"And the baker has confirmed your pink cake," I said.

"Our day is going to be so special." Margie said, overcome with excitement.

Growing up, I'd dreamed of finding someone to love who'd show me the same affection Vrok did for Margie, not the stilted coldness my parents displayed to each other—and most of the time, me.

In my teen years, I'd spent so much time drawing wedding gowns and picturing venues, plus making sketches and lists of what would make up the perfect wedding, it made sense for me to study hospitality management and business in college. After that, I got my certification and opened my business, only to have Love & Lace, my ex's chain wedding planner company, use our relationship to undercut my prices. He shouldered me out of business, and I had no choice but to set up shop somewhere new.

I hated to think Raze could be planning to do the same thing.

A town the size of Monsterville could support two wedding planners. He needed to learn how to share.

"Is there anything else?" Margie asked, standing. "I've got a gown fitting appointment in ten minutes."

I'd made the arrangements. "No, that should be it for now. I'll reach out with any questions."

"Thank you."

"I'll let you know how the fitting goes," Margie said as she and Vrok started toward the front door.

"Take pictures," I called out after them.

"No pictures," Vrok said. "Not today, that is."

"I told you this was what I wanted," Margie ground out. They stopped near Raze, who watched them, his head snapping back and forth like this was a prime tennis match and he had a front row seat.

"If you're not willing to let the photographer take pictures today, I'm calling it quits," Margie said.

"Really?" Vrok's thick brow drew together, and his spine stiffened. His dragonette fluttered its wings before settling. "You'd do something like that?"

"Vrok?" Margie bellowed.

"Yes?" He held his spine tight. I had to hand it to him, he had the stiff upper lip he'd need with Margie.

She wrenched off the ring from her left finger and threw it at him. It smacked his chest before falling, clinking on the tile floor. "We're over."

With that, she stormed from the room.

Vrok forlornly looked from me to Raze before stooping down to pick up the ring. "I'm sorry. I guess . . . the wedding's off. I'll, um . . . You can keep the deposit." He eased around Raze and left.

Damn. I slumped back in my seat. One job gone, just like that.

Raze huffed. "He's better off without her, I think."

I saw red.

Standing, I rounded my desk and marched right up to Raze. "Why are you inside my office?" It was a struggle not to drool over his chiseled jawline and thick thighs. Why couldn't I shrug off my crush?

"Way to go with Margie and Vrok."

"Don't rub it in, though you're right that it's probably for the best." I wrenched my hair off my face and resecured it at my nape in the ponytail I'd made this morning it kept slipping out of. "Tell me what you want."

"Is that the way to greet a friend?" he asked in a sardonic, lofty tone. "We have something to discuss." Brushing past me, he took the chair Vrok had just vacated.

With a sigh deflating my lungs, I followed, sitting behind my desk once more.

My phone chimed, and I scowled at it before scrolling into the text message. Grr. It was from Harris, my ex.

I want you back, he texted. *I miss you. Can we talk?*

No, I quickly replied. *Leave me alone forever.* I turned off my phone and shoved it into a drawer.

"Welcome," I told Raze with pretend cheer. "What brings you here today, Raze?"

"I have a proposition for you," he said in a grumbly-growly voice that should make irritation flash through me. Instead, it made me long to drape myself across a bed—naked—while he climbed all over me.

"What might that be?" I asked, cocking my head.

"Someone's put in a low bid on the fae royal wedding."

"You *didn't*," I fumed, slamming my fist on my desk.

He huffed. "I'd like to get the job as much as you, but my bid will be honest."

I flopped back in my chair. "We're the only wedding planners in town. Who put in the other bid?"

"Love & Lace."

My damn ex's company. With branches all over the state, he could toss out low bids and spread the loss across the entire business.

I was sunk. There was no way I'd win this important job and after losing Margie and Vrok's wedding, I was going to need to eat ramen for the rest of the month.

"He . . ." I blinked hard, trying not to cry. How could my ex do this? I loved Monsterville. I didn't want to move again.

I wanted to snap at Raze for watching me with a sardonic gleam in his eyes, but I held it inside. It wasn't his fault. There was no need to snarl at him. I'd save that for my ex.

"So, Elisa," Raze said. "What would you think of combining our businesses?"

Get Uptown Ogre Now!